MIKE
KNOWLES

ROCKS

BEAT

PAPER

Printing: Marquis   5   4   3   2   1
Printed and bound in Canada

Published by ECW Press
665 Gerrard Street East
Toronto, on M4M 1Y2
416-694-3348 / info@ecwpress.com

LIBRARY AND ARCHIVES CANADA
CATALOGUING IN PUBLICATION

Knowles, Mike, author
Rocks beat paper / Mike Knowles.

(A Wilson mystery)
Issued in print and electronic formats.
ISBN 978-1-77041-101-2 (paperback)
ISBN 978-1-77305-030-0 (PDF)
ISBN 978-1-77305-029-4 (epub)

I. Title. II. Series: Knowles, Mike. Wilson mystery.

PS8621.N67R63 2017   C813'.6   C2016-906386-0

C2016-906387-9

Cover design: David Gee
Cover image: © Logan Zillmer/
Trevillion Images
Interior image: blood spatter
© itchySan/iStockphoto

The publication of *Rocks Beat Paper* has been generously supported by the Canada Council for the Arts, which last year invested $153 million to bring the arts to Canadians throughout the country, and by the Government of Canada through the Canada Book Fund. *Nous remercions le Conseil des arts du Canada de son soutien. L'an dernier, le Conseil a investi 153 millions de dollars pour mettre de l'art dans la vie des Canadiennes et des Canadiens de tout le pays. Ce livre est financé en partie par le gouvernement du Canada.* We also acknowledge the support of the Ontario Arts Council (OAC), an agency of the Government of Ontario, which last year funded 1,737 individual artists and 1,095 organizations in 223 communities across Ontario for a total of $52.1 million, and the contribution of the Government of Ontario through the Ontario Book Publishing Tax Credit and the Ontario Media Development Corporation.

FOR ANDREA.

It could be for no one else.

CHAPTER ONE

I couldn't stop thinking about the circus. My parents took me once when I was a kid. It was a travelling circus; the kind that pulls into the city one morning and transforms a stadium into a big top. I sat in a bucket seat craning my neck as I tried to take in everything that was happening under the bright unflinching glare of the mounted lights. This was thirty years ago and the performers were all Russian. The lion on the pedestal was underfed and the whip that whistled through the air made contact with leathered scars that no one in the audience gave a hint of a shit about. I saw maybe twenty seconds of the entire lion act through the porthole of space created by a hand resting on a hip. The adult standing in front of me had decided the circus was too exciting to take in seated, but not so exciting that her feet found themselves overwhelmed. The tall woman sagged in every possible place, and her body had the same contours as a beanbag chair. By moving side to side at opportune moments, I was able to see a half minute of the elephant and most of the trapeze acts. Then the little boy beside the woman convinced her to put him up on her shoulders so he could see even more of what I was missing. The newly erected tower of humans offered me a small window with a view of the clowns. Six men came out from behind the curtain and feigned panic at the sight of the emaciated bear. The sight of the clowns sent people in droves to the concession stands and washrooms. The clowns, obviously used to the mass exodus, upped their game and began loudly honking horns. When they did manage to turn a head their way, it never lasted. I had been holding it through the last two acts, but there was no way I was leaving — I could finally see the show and I wasn't about to get up.

The clowns were all variations of the same tramp. They fluctuated in height and weight, but the cheap costumes and sloppy makeup were the same. I saw every tumble and every prank without having to navigate my way around a constantly shifting human obstruction. Near the end of the act, two of the clowns disappeared behind a curtain and returned less than a minute later in the front seat of a compact car. I remember thinking the car must have been European because I had never seen one on the road before. All six clowns surrounded the vehicle and began vaulting one another over the hood. The lingering disinterested crowd managed only a few weak *oohs* and *ahs* for the acrobatics. Everyone shut their mouth when the bear came over. The trainer, at the behest of the clown who had been behind the wheel of the compact, led the animal to the car; he opened the door and pointed to the interior. After a few sharp commands that echoed in the silent stadium, the bear wedged his bony ribs through the door and into the car.

The audience responded with the sound of creaks as they got out of their chairs. What came next surprised everyone. The clowns opened the three remaining doors and began to get inside. I got out of my seat and strained to see how the clowns, who already had little chance of fitting inside the car, managed to do it with a bear in the front seat. The doors began to close one by one. When the final door slammed shut, the sound was met with an eruption of applause.

It was that car, at least a decade old thirty years ago, I was thinking about while I watched the front door. How many people were going to walk through that entrance? I had counted seven in the last hour. The meet had been scheduled for nine, by my watch a half hour ago, and people just kept showing up. A couple of guys had been early; most were late. I was late to the meeting myself, but not late to the house. I had been in the neighbourhood at four and in a parking space with a view of the house at five. The townhouse was in Jersey City on the quiet end of a busy street. Someone was home. Through the open blinds, I saw movement every few minutes. At seven p.m., a Volkswagen pulled into the driveway and a man got out and walked to the trunk. He yanked out numerous grocery bags and worked to get them all into his hands. He managed to lug all of the bags up the stairs to the front door. Rather than put the bags down, the man chose to kick the door. Porch lights came on and a woman opened the front door. The man sidestepped his way into the townhouse and used his heel to close the door behind him. After that, the house was a buzz of energy. Lights went on in every room and people moved quickly around the house. At eight thirty, a pickup pulled into the remaining half of the driveway. A man got out and strode the steps to the door. He was easily a head taller than the cab of the truck. He spent less than a minute on the porch before the door opened and he ducked his way under the door and into the house. In the foyer, the tall man paused to hug the guy who had brought in the groceries. I caught a second of his profile, but it was enough. The hug lasted long enough to make these two men partners, not the life kind — the job kind. The hug ended with simultaneous back claps and then the shorter of the two men closed the door.

Ten to nine brought another man; this one parked down the street and didn't need to duck to cross the threshold. The third guest also wasn't greeted with a hug from the man who clearly fulfilled the role of host. The next six guests arrived in an order that could only be described as random. The intervals and appearance resisted any form of pattern, but the numbers woke something paranoid in my brain. The binoculars put the monster back in the cage. Too many of the interactions were stiff — far too stiff for men who knew each other. Had these men been on the job, they would have been on the job. No one would be shaking hello if they were getting down to the business of killing someone who was about to show up.

My plan had been to walk in five minutes after the last man showed up. The problem: the last man never seemed to show. People kept walking up to the townhouse, making awkward introductions, and walking inside.

The eighth man came from the busier end of the street. He wore a wool pea coat and a scarf knotted around his neck. The dark hair pushed back by the brisk March air never lost its shape. Even in the wind it looked cool. He effortlessly shifted his hips and glided around an elderly woman doing her best to keep her grocery cart from tipping over. She forgot about the rickety cart and the wind when she passed the man on the street. The old woman stopped on the sidewalk and turned her head to follow the ass of the much younger man. Through the binoculars, I watched the man's face as he gave a small wave to the woman he knew was staring at his back. Miles was smiling ear to ear.

I had worked a job with Miles more than two years back. We had made money, but not friends. Miles let the smile dim a few watts as he turned up the path to the door. He knocked and was let inside. There was a handshake, but this one wasn't awkward; it wasn't that Miles and the Volkswagen driver were acquainted — Miles just didn't do anything awkward. I saw Miles's mouth move rapidly, and suddenly the host seemed uncomfortable. He directed Miles with a wave of his hand and closed the door.

I checked my watch as I unbuckled my seat belt. The numbers were unusual, to say the least, but nothing else read as dangerous. I got out of the car and felt the cold spring air collide with my exposed neck. I ignored the chill and checked the street for traffic before walking to the other side. I angled my approach and stepped up onto the sidewalk a few feet from the path Miles had taken a few minutes before. No one watched me from the windows as I walked towards the house. I stopped at the door and checked the street again before knocking twice. Half a minute later, the door swung open.

"Yes?" Up close, I could see that the host was in the less fun end of his thirties. His stomach pushed against the buttons of his shirt and his belt was just holding on to the last hole.

"I'm here for the meeting," I said.

"Name?"

"Wilson."

The host's face stretched into a smile that exposed straight white teeth. He extended a hand and gave my own a vigorous shake.

"Name's David. It's really great to meet you. My brother-in-law told me all about you. You did a job together eight months back. You remember Alvin, right?"

"'Course he does."

I turned my head and saw the man who had been forced to duck as he entered the townhouse. This time I had more than just a second's look at his profile.

"Alvin," I said.

"How many times I gotta tell ya? I'm goin' by Vin now."

"Right," I said. "Everybody here?"

"We're still waiting on someone," David said. "But that's cool, there's beer and snacks downstairs. Make yourself at home."

I looked at David. He was serious; there were snacks in the basement. I looked at Alvin, but he just nodded and turned towards the stairs. He hunched his shoulders in anticipation of the slanted ceiling and led the way down the stairs. I stepped onto the basement carpet and immediately saw a pool table and a large flat-screen mounted on the far wall. The television was so large I could make out the stats scrolling underneath the game. Folding chairs had been scattered against the walls throughout the basement. The pool table occupied two other men and the couch across from the TV was at capacity; three men had squeezed themselves in to watch college basketball. Miles ignored both games and set up shop alone at a card table.

He saw me and nodded. "Do you think this is a rumpus room?" He said as he ran his hand back and forth across the felt-covered table. "I have no idea what a rumpus room is, but I think I might be sitting in one. I have no facts to back it up. It's more of a gut feeling."

One of the men at the pool table paused midshot and gave Miles a hard stare. The pool player was big — big shoulders, big hands, big gut. Even the hair that wasn't saddled by the old baseball cap was big. The curly and wild locks passed his ears and deformed the shadow of his head on the worn tabletop.

Miles followed my line of sight to the man. "Oh, did I do it again? You were shooting weren't you? Sorry. I'll try to be more quiet."

I circled the table and took a seat that allowed me to keep my back to the wall.

"You're late," Miles said.

I looked over the bowls of chips that surrounded a warm shrimp ring. I had never been to a meeting with a shrimp ring before. "A lot of people here," I said.

Miles nodded. "A lot of people in a rumpus room."

"How many times are you going to say rumpus room?" the pool player barked.

"Depends," Miles said. "Do you think this is a rumpus

room? If you're sure it's not, then I'll definitely stop saying it. I don't want to sound like an idiot."

The pool player muttered something loud enough for everyone to hear and went back to his game. Miles ignored the insult and turned his head back to me. He smirked and then his face lost all trace of expression. "You have a problem with the numbers?"

I nodded. "Every man you add to a job adds more than just a pair of hands. It adds baggage. All the personalities and ideas create variables, layers of unexpected consequences that will need to be dealt with. Every job has something, and you deal with them as they come. Most times you can because an isolated problem isn't usually enough to sink a job. But every number you add expands the potential fuckups and makes them exponentially harder to solve because you have to work out a solution that makes the whole group happy. I see eight men walk through a door and I get a headache just thinking about the homework."

"What the fuck are you talking about?"

The pool player wasn't playing pool anymore. He was standing beside the table with the cue in two hands. Seeing the man bent over the table didn't give me a real impression of his size. I had pegged him as big. Standing at full height suddenly made the word feel weak — the man was huge. His white T-shirt hugged his barrel-shaped torso; the logo on the old shirt had faded into an indecipherable smear that matched the grey streaks running through his tangled hair. His heavy hands wrung the cue, and the motion revealed prison ink on the inside of his forearms. The tattoo was faded and poorly done, likely from his first fall a long way back. Based on his eagerness to fight in order to cement his position as the alpha in the room, I guessed he did more than one stretch.

I nodded my head towards Miles while keeping my eyes on the man holding the cue. "I'm talking to him," I said.

"Your *talking* is fucking up my game."

"That's because we're all crammed down here in this rumpus room."

The big man brought the cue up in a single hand and pointed it at Miles's head. "What did I say about your mouth?"

Behind him, the other pool player had given up on the game. He was taller than the other man, but slim in every way his opponent was immense.

Miles opened his mouth to say something and then gave up on it. He turned his head towards me. "You said you watched eight men walk through the door. I just caught that. You weren't late, you were just on the fence."

"Not so much on the fence now that I see the workload," I said.

"Too much homework?"

I nodded. "A nine-man job is worse than calculus."

"What about a job with nine men and a woman? What subject is that?"

I followed Miles's nod and watched a black woman take the last two steps down into the basement.

The pool player forgot about us. "What the fuck is this? Tony, you seeing this shit?"

The other pool player said, "I see it, Johnny." Tony had a deep southern drawl that matched the mullet trailing down his neck.

"What the fuck we need a nigger for?"

"She-nigger," Tony added.

If the woman on the stairs heard the two men, and there was no way she could have missed it, she didn't let it show. She stopped at the bottom of the stairs and gave the basement a slow once-over. After considering her seating options, she selected a spot on the far side of the card table next to Miles.

The second her ass made full contact with the seat, Miles leaned in. "Let me ask you something."

The petite woman stopped scanning the room and turned her eyes to Miles. She had a face made for the table she was seated at — pure poker. Her eyes had the dull interest of a woman who had heard it all before and had sat through the re-runs.

Johnny jabbed the cue towards Miles. "I swear to God, if you say rumpus room . . ." He let the threat linger in the ether.

"What the hell is a rumpus room?" the woman said.

"I think this might be a rumpus room," Miles said. "No one else seems to have an opinion on the subject though."

The woman looked around the basement. Her gaze lingered a little longer on Johnny and Tony. "I'm not sure there's enough room to rumpus."

Johnny crossed the room, jolting the table violently with his hip as he passed. He took a handful of shirt and pulled Miles's face to his.

"What did I tell you?"

"Alright, everybody, it looks like everyone is here, so how about we get started?" Alvin was at the bottom of the stairs, looking our way. "We got a lot to talk about and no time for this shit."

Johnny held onto Miles long enough for him to feel like he hadn't lost any face, and then he let him go.

David came down the stairs a second later, a laptop under his arm, and walked around Alvin to the television. "Sorry, guys, I have to turn this off."

One of the guys on the couch said, "Just mute it."

David looked apologetic. "Can't. We need it for the presentation." He fiddled with a long remote and the basketball game became a black screen. After a few seconds at the keyboard, the TV mirrored the laptop display.

"Pull the chairs around," Alvin said.

When the five of us didn't move from the table, Alvin said, "There a problem here?"

"There's an asshole here," Johnny said.

Miles leaned in towards the woman. "He means me."

She let an eyebrow lazily creep up about half an inch. "I gathered that."

"See what I mean," Johnny said. "He won't fucking stop. Maybe if there were a few less teeth in that mouth of his, he'd be a bit more careful about opening it."

Alvin sighed. "We don't got time for this. You want to hear about the job, find a seat. You want to pick a fight, get the hell out of here and find a fucking bar."

"I don't know about you, but I want to stay," Miles said.

Johnny looked at Tony. His partner returned the look with one of his own. There was some kind of communication in the exchange that only the two men understood. Whatever wasn't said was enough to convince Johnny to stay and hear Alvin out. He stepped in close to Miles and jabbed a finger into his chest. "Just keep to the other side of the room."

The two men walked away from the table and found two chairs against one of the walls. The woman gave the two men a head start before she got up, pushed her chair back into place, and found a chair far away from Johnny and Tony.

When it was just the two of us, I looked Miles in the eye. "Why are you here?"

"Same reason as you."

"I'm here to work," I said.

"Same goes for me."

"That what you're doing?"

"What? Those guys are assholes."

"Those guys are here for the job."

"So?"

"So the job is only the job if it gets done. That can't happen if you get murdered with a pool cue in the middle of a rumpus room."

Miles clapped me on the shoulder. "So you do think this is a rumpus room."

"Don't know. That makes two things I don't know."

"What's the other thing?"

"If this is the only job you're working," I said.

Miles went a beat without saying anything. It was long enough for me to let a bit of a grin form on my face and for him to rebound.

"You really comfortable with guys like that watching your back?"

I looked over the group of men as I considered my response. Alvin had gotten to his feet and was giving the room a once-over of his own. He worked hard to catch my eye, but I gave his stare the slip. "You want to work with upstanding citizens, go be a bank teller. The background checks weed out most of the riff-raff. Right now, you're not in a bank, you're in a basement with nine criminals. We're all riff-raff. You're sitting around hassling two guys because you think they're not decent human beings. Your only concern should be if they can do what they say they can do. If they can do that, everything else they say gets a pass."

"So you want me to give them a pass?"

"I want you to shut your mouth and keep your feelings to yourself because every time you piss them off you take their minds off the job and put the rest of us in a bit more shit."

"You really sticking up for that white-power asshole?"

I nodded. "You want a noble thief, get a library card."

Alvin gave up on being subtle and spoke loud enough to be heard over the rest of the conversations going on. "We ready to get started?"

Miles ignored the question; he had one of his own for me. "Do you really think you can trust those two to watch your back?"

I looked over at Johnny and Tony and found them staring at me. I stared back until I got bored. It happened fast. "My back doesn't need watching. I just need them to do what they say they'll do."

"And you think they can?"

I looked back at the two thugs. "I'm going to find out."

CHAPTER TWO

"**I** just want to start things out by saying thank you to everybody for making it out here tonight." Alvin's head was just low enough to escape scraping against the drop ceiling. The inch or so of clearance should have made him cautious, but he moved without any apprehension or concern. He was comfortable in the basement, and, by association, comfortable with David. He went on. "My name is Vin, and I'm the one who reached out to all of you."

"So this is your job?" The question came from one of the men on the couch. He was a short paunchy man with skin the colour of tanned leather.

"Mine and David's. David is my brother-in-law," Alvin said. "The job was his idea. He told me about it, I gave him some input, and we partnered up."

Another question from the man on the couch. "So, he's a citizen."

"Yeah, but he's family and I vouch for him. You can trust David. More importantly, you can trust the job. I've been over it a bunch of times and it's got one hell of a payout."

"It's going to have to. There are ten people here." This came from the couch, but not from the same man. He was seated beside the first speaker and shared the man's features and stature, but not his age. The second man was much younger. The heavy mustache he wore showed no signs of the grey evident in the other man's stubble.

I pegged the two men as blood relatives. The age difference made father and son a knee-jerk assumption, but I dismissed it. The younger man showed no deference to the other man when he spoke his mind. Conversely, he showed no sign of disrespect to his counterpart when he spoke out either. He wasn't petulantly trying to assert himself into the conversation to prove he was an equal — he was an equal. The relationship wasn't paternal; it was fraternal.

"Look, I know everybody has their concerns. Let's save them until the end. Hear David out and then decide what you think. Okay?"

There were a couple of grunts from around the room that Alvin chose to interpret as agreement. He moved away from the television, and his brother-in-law took his place.

"Before I get started, I want to remind everyone that there is beer and food if you want it."

"It's not a PTA meeting," the older man on the couch said. When he spoke, he didn't check the room to see if others shared his opinion. It was a play for dominance — a challenge to the two men who had called the meeting. I wasn't sure if all the chest beating was intentional, or just a knee-jerk reaction. You put enough rough men in a room, there's going to be friction. I sighed. Counting the alphas was just more homework.

"Diego, is it?" David asked.

Both men on the couch said, "Yes," at the same time.

"I'm sorry," David said. "I'm confused. I meant him." David gestured with his chin towards the older of the two men. "You're Diego, right?"

The older of the two men nodded.

"Right," David said. "Got it." He focused on the younger man. "So, he's Diego, and you're —"

"Diego."

David laughed. "Diego."

The man nodded.

"You're both named Diego?"

"Si," the older Diego said. I labelled him Diego #1. "It was our father's name." There was steel in his voice. It was the kind of steel that had been forged from repeated fights over the subject. "Is there a problem?" David flushed instantly. "No, it's just — I just —"

On the couch, the two men broke into wide smiles that exposed an abundance of white teeth. "I'm just kidding. I know it's fucked up."

David's flush bloomed and began to fade. "It's really fucked." The chuckle he had managed to generate died in his throat.

"Hey, we get to say that. He was our father. You, on the other hand, are calling our legacy fucked, gringo."

The room went quiet for a few seconds before David pointed at Diego #1 and let out a laugh. "You're messing with me again, right?"

"No," Diego #1 said. "I most definitely am not. Now why don't you get on with what you turned off the basketball game to say before you really step in it?"

"Okay," David said. "We can do the rest of the introductions later." He clicked the mouse and an image of a red-brick building appeared. "This is Mendelson Jewels. I work at Mendelson as a jewellery designer."

"Never heard of it," Johnny said from his side of the room. It was his turn to piss on the carpet and mark his territory.

"Few have," David agreed. "Mendelson's clients are very wealthy and very private. There are a number of celebrities who buy pieces from us exclusively."

"Anyone we'd know?" Johnny asked.

David said a name and Johnny screwed up his face in thought. "Never heard of her."

"I know her," Miles said. "She won an Oscar."

"And wore Mendelson on the red carpet."

"I saw that, too," Miles said.

"Shocker," Johnny called across the small space.

Miles opened his mouth, but he shut it when I shook my head.

"We operate by appointment only, and we make everything in-house."

"That must put a lot of diamonds in one place," Diego #1 said.

"Not as a rule. Often we buy specifically for commissions. But this month is different."

"Different how?" Diego #1 asked.

"There is a new movie festival at the end of the month. You probably heard about it."

Miles nodded and Johnny snorted.

David went on. "The Central Park Movie Festival was set up by a group of A-list Hollywood players, and it has received an unbelievable amount of press. I doubt there will be a movie star left in L.A. while it's going on. That kind of presence has put a huge demand on us for pieces to sell and loan. The studio safes will be loaded for the next month."

"How much are we talking about?" Johnny asked.

"Ballpark — ten million."

"Holy shit," Johnny said.

"Big pie," Diego said. "But there are a lot of slices to cut."

"A mill apiece," Tony said. "That's still a hell of a score."

I watched Johnny count the bodies in the room and nod when he confirmed his partner's math.

Diego #1 shook his head. "That million apiece still needs to be fenced, cowboy. We rob Hollywood, and the score will be so hot you'll need sunglasses just to look at it. The fence will know that and he'll charge for it. Suddenly a million ain't a million anymore."

Tony's face reddened. He didn't like being made to look like a fool. "Still a hell of a score."

"Maybe," Diego #1 said.

Diego #2 leaned forward. "You got a fence lined up?"

David nodded.

Diego looked unconvinced. "You got a guy who can move ten million in stones?"

David shook his head. "I have three men willing to fence what we take. Between them, the cost is not an issue."

"And what will it take to hire these three men with deep pockets?" Diego #1 asked.

"Thirty percent," David said.

"Fuck that," Johnny said. "We're supposed to be the ones doing the robbing. Thirty! We're talking about moving diamonds, not nuclear weapons."

"The kind of people who can move this calibre of product aren't running street-corner shops. They're big players taking on a great deal of risk."

"You tell me who these guys are, and I'll get them down to a reasonable cut," Johnny said.

"I — I don't think that's wise."

"And losing thirty percent is? Listen, maybe this is something you should let a pro handle. It's not like buying a car."

David opened his mouth to say something, but he couldn't find the words.

Johnny pressed him again. "You know I'm right."

David, mouth still open, looked at his brother-in-law.

Alvin leaned forward and let his elbows rest on his knees. "The kind of weight we're talking about moving has to be done by people in David's line of work. We need to work through them, and they won't work through you."

Johnny snorted. "Yeah, we'll see about that. You give me their names and see how long we're losing thirty."

Diego #1 lifted his hands. "We're getting ahead of ourselves. We need to hear how this job is going to work before we start arguing about how to cash out."

"You're right," David said. He seemed happy to get off the topic of fencing the diamonds. He clicked the laptop keyboard, and the TV displayed a new image of the brick building. There was no sign posted out front; the only identifying markers were a few brass numbers posted above the door, an intercom, and a security camera.

"Can you zoom in on those?" The question came from a man on the couch. He was a third of the men on the couch, but he occupied close to half the space. He was midforties in age and in the high two hundreds in weight. His girth filled out an extra-large sweater that had pilled in almost every conceivable place. The rough sweater had collected a bounty of hair, dirt, and crumbs that rivaled the bathroom floor of an hourly rate motel.

"Yes, I have more shots of that. Just give me a second." David opened a folder on his desktop and I noticed the high number of images it contained. He scrolled through the file folder until he found the thumbnail he was interested in. A close-up of the surveillance camera popped up on the television screen. The man crowding the couch leaned forward and peered at the new image through dirty wire-rimmed glasses. "And the intercom?"

David went back to the laptop, and a few seconds later the camera was replaced by an ornate keypad. Everyone watched who had to be our tech guy as he looked over the screen. He scrutinized the picture before using his hands on his knees to wedge himself back against the couch cushions.

"Can you also show me the computer that the camera and intercom feed into? I'll also need to see the router and where the hard lines are located."

"Fuck, I am going to fall asleep," Johnny said. "Can we save the geek talk until the end?"

"That okay with you, Elliot?" Alvin asked.

"Yes, it's okay with Elliot," Johnny said. He answered with the kind of assurance that could only be gained after a lifetime of pushing guys like Elliot around. "Take us inside."

The next slide was of the door. "The door is wired into the alarm, obviously, and it's heavy. Saul had it custom made. Everything is custom made."

"You have keys?" Diego #1 asked.

Everyone looked at him.

"Not a stupid question," he said.

"Only Saul has keys," David said.

"Alarm passcode?"

David shook his head.

"Our *inside man* doesn't seem to be so inside. How about we just call him 'man'?"

"Keep going, David," Alvin said.

"Beyond the door is reception. There is another door there leading to the showroom." David clicked the keypad and we saw a small waiting room with a desk on one side and two couches and a coffee table on the other.

"That other door like the first?" Diego #1 asked.

David nodded.

"Can the receptionist open the doors?"

David said, "Yes, she can use her computer to see who is outside. Once she verifies who they are over the intercom, she lets them in and contacts Saul. When he's ready, she buzzes them through to the showroom."

David tapped the computer keyboard and the showroom appeared. The dark hardwood floor reflected the light from the glass cases positioned around the room. I counted four cases arranged in a long C shape: one for bracelets, one for necklaces, one for earrings, and a final longer case for rings.

Everyone in the room was quiet while they took in the images. The cases weren't packed — if anything, they were sparse — but the limited number of items inside the cases were spectacular. The work was intricate and the materials opulent and expensive. The pieces were impressive, but so were the cases. Diego #1 noticed the latter almost right away.

"That a keypad on the case?"

David nodded. "The hinges have pneumatic motors built into them. If you key in the correct numbers, the cases will open themselves. Plus, the glass is —"

"Custom," Miles said.

"I'm told," David said, "that they can take a bullet without shattering."

"So how do we get into them?" Johnny asked. "Do you have the codes for the cases, or does our resident Poindexter have to open each one?"

Elliot ignored the insult. "It could be done if time wasn't an issue. Is time an issue?"

David shrugged. "We have all night."

A few people nodded their heads.

"Provided," David added, "the security system was dealt with first."

"So we have to find our way around the doors and the cases," Diego #1 said. "Any other problems we need to know about?"

"We still need to talk about the security guards," David said.

"Holy shit," Diego #1 said. "Guards, too?"

"Could be worse," Miles said. "I thought he was going to say there was a moat."

"Mendelson's doesn't employ on-site guards at night," David said. "But, there is a security company contracted to do nightly rounds. They aren't exclusive to Mendelson; they cover a number of other jewellers in the area as well. I timed his route out. We have fifteen minutes between passes. If we can get in without setting off the alarm, there won't be any problems."

"There is a problem," Diego #1 said. "If that alarm gets disabled, that security guard will check the premises."

"They'll put a call in to your boss, too," Diego #2 added. "So even if we stay quiet, there's no guarantee someone won't come down and check inside."

"I agree," David said. "It sounds bad. That's why we found someone who could handle the computers."

Everyone looked at Elliot. He gave it some thought before he opened his mouth. "You having access to everything inside means we could run a program that would let me inside remotely. Then, we can rig the system so that it doesn't register the alarm."

David sighed. "I don't have access to the security room. We have two security guards in the store, and one is responsible for monitoring the store cameras. They walk in with Saul in the morning and they leave with him at night. There is no time that I could get inside."

"He has to pee sometime," Miles said.

David nodded. "He locks the room when he does. And don't say eating because he does that at his desk."

"Two guards seem like overkill. One is basically watching the other one work," Diego #1 said.

It wasn't overkill. It was something else. "One guard is

for the customers," I said. "The other one is for the staff."

Every head turned to look at me. From the expression on David's face, I could tell I was right.

"'Bout time you said something," Miles said. "I was beginning to think you fell asleep."

"You're right," David said. "Let me backtrack a bit. I've been working for Saul Mendelson for twenty years. I was his apprentice, and it was always his plan for me to take over the business from him when he was ready to retire."

"You two have a difference of opinion on the date?" Miles asked.

"Saul should have retired over a year ago. That had been the plan. But something happened. He changed. He forgets things. He'll lose track of order dates or where he left his tools. He confuses dates. He'll talk to me about pieces for customers who died years ago, but it's clear he thinks they're still alive. And recently, he's become paranoid. And mean. He accuses the staff of stealing, he's suspicious of the customers, he even sometimes thinks I'm out to get him."

"To be fair," Miles said, "you are trying to rip him off."

"I have no choice," David said. "The business is starting to lose momentum. It still makes a hell of a lot of money. Saul hired talented people and taught them things they could never have learned anywhere else. Plus, we still have name recognition and a client list that other jewellers would kill for."

"So what's the problem?" Diego #1 said.

"We're just rolling forward — it's all momentum. There is nothing driving us. If anything, Saul is putting on the brakes. Last month, he fired two jewellers with twenty-five years' experience between them. He didn't replace them. Yesterday, he forgot they were gone. He was screaming about how they were late to work and about how this generation has no respect for what they do. He was ready to fire them all over again before I reminded him that he already had. We are barely keeping up with demand right now. Everything has been delayed at least twice, and the clients are talking refunds. I tried to talk to Saul, but all he wanted to talk about was another jeweller who he is sure is stealing from the business. If we lose another body, there will be another round of delays and it will mark the beginning of the end for us."

"If everything is behind, why is the take so high?" Diego #1 asked. It was a good question.

David ran a hand through his hair. "That's the one and only upside for us. Supply has nothing to do with demand. He's been ordering stones and metals every month. Sometimes twice a month. He's stuck in a loop; he's convinced it's 2005."

"That a good year for jewellery?" Miles asked.

"It was a good year for Saul. A couple of A-list celebrities, real A-list celebrities, wore his work on the red carpet. And they said his name to Joan Rivers, to *Access Hollywood*, and to *Entertainment Tonight*. The very next day we were inundated with orders."

"What A-listers?" Miles asked.

David said two names that made an impression on everyone in the room except for me.

Johnny was the first to recover. "So, he's buying diamonds?"

"Raw diamonds," David said.

"Where is he keeping them?"

David busied himself with the laptop; a few seconds later the image on the screen was replaced with a picture of a safe. "He keeps them in these."

"How many?" Diego #1 asked.

"Two," David said. "One in back and another in Saul's office. That one there is Saul's. I managed to get a shot of it when Saul stormed out to berate the security guard about his inability to catch employees stealing from him."

"They look heavy duty," Johnny said.

David said something, but I ignored it. I was watching the Diegos. Both men eyed the screen with a level of attention they never gave the basketball game. Diego #2 pulled his gaze away from the television to put on a pair of glasses. As soon as he had the eyewear on, his eyes were back on the screen.

"That Italian?" Diego #2 asked. The question wasn't for David. It was for his brother.

Diego #1 shook his head. "Look at the dial."

Diego #2 squinted. "Swiss."

"Uh hunh."

"Shit."

"Uh hunh."

"What?" Johnny asked. "They extra hard to open or something?"

"Take more than a can opener," Diego #2 said.

"Couple of hours with a diamond-tipped drill bit and a scope would get us a look at the change hole. 'Course, I'd want to see the specs first."

"We'd have to go in through the side," Diego #2 said.

His brother nodded. "For sure. No other way with something like that, but I'd rather know the sweet spot than waste time groping around."

"What about using a torch?" Johnny said.

"I've seen it done," Tony said.

"Maybe with some box you found in a bedroom closet. You can't cut into something like this."

"Why not?" Tony asked.

"They layer the metals. They put a layer of stainless steel behind the heavier gage layers. The combination makes cutting in impossible. You just get a headache from the smell and the fucking light," Diego #1 said.

"Maybe you should use something a little stronger," Johnny said.

"Something louder," Tony added.

Diego #1 pointed at the screen. "That box right there is a high-maintenance piece of ass. You want inside, you need to push her buttons just right. You need to seduce her nice and slow. That's the only way to get her to open her door."

"What the fuck does that mean?"

Diego #2 pulled his eyes away from the TV screen. "What it means is you can't blow open a safe like that. That's not some commercial safe that people use to keep their mother's wedding ring away from a burglar. That safe is seriously heavy duty. Inside the door is a pane of glass. If the glass shatters, from something like an explosion, the inner bolts will slide into place and lock it up tight. That's why we need the drill and the scope. We need to get around that glass."

"How long would something like that take?" David asked.

Diego #1 said, "With the right tools and a look at the specs — a couple hours."

"Total?"

"Each," Diego #2 said.

"So, two hours," David said.

Diego #1 shook his head. "Four."

"I don't get it. Two hours a safe. Two men. Two safes. Two hours."

Diego #1 shook his head. "I need my brother working with me. He has to monitor the glass while I work the drill. I make a wrong move and that thing will turn into the world's most expensive paperweight."

"So best-case scenario, we're inside for four hours," Tony said.

"That's without any complications," Diego #1 said. "And when have you ever worked a job that didn't have complications?"

Johnny dug huge fingers through the curly nest of hair on his head. "What's our window?"

David was quick to answer. "Saul leaves with security at eight o'clock every night."

"A twelve-hour window is a good stretch. A man could get a lot done in twelve hours," Johnny said. He aimed a sneer at the woman sitting on the opposite side of the room. "No offense."

Miles leaned towards the woman next to him. "Is he insulting your gender or your productivity?"

The woman laughed.

"What did I tell you about that mouth?"

Miles smiled. "You said I couldn't say rumpus room. You never mentioned anything about what I could do with my mouth."

"Add keeping it shut to the list."

Miles opened his mouth to say something, but I spoke first. A fight would derail the conversation.

"When is the film festival?" I asked.

"The end of the month. It runs through the last week, and on the Sunday there is a huge gala to close it all."

"Saul has us working overtime on new pieces that no one has seen invoices for. As designers finish up their dresses, there will be some legitimate orders coming in, but not as many as Saul envisions. After that, the business will quiet down for a while."

"Run the slideshow again," I said.

David nodded, likely relieved for the break from the spotlight.

One by one, the images made a second appearance. I saw the door, the waiting room, the showroom, and the backroom from numerous angles and distances. Interspersed were a few good shots of the security office and the cameras positioned around the store; emphasis was placed on the safes and the glass cases containing the custom-made jewellery.

"How did you get all of these?" I asked.

"My phone. It took me nearly a month to get them all. I had to time it just right. When the guard left his room to use the washroom, I took two shots. I never got greedy, and I never got caught."

I nodded. "I didn't see another door. Fire codes should demand a fire exit."

David paused. "There's a door," he said. "It's in the back next to the security office. I didn't take any pictures of it because there's nothing to see. Saul had the door custom made. There are no hinges exposed, and it's heavily reinforced. On top of that, there's an apartment building looking down on that side of the store. I figured any noise out there would put too many eyes on us. I can't see it as our way in."

"We need pictures of it," I said. "You might not see it as our way in, but it might be our way out."

"I never thought of it that way."

"That's why you brought us on."

David nodded. "Okay, I can get shots of the door."

"Where does all the work get done? I only saw one office."

"That was mine," David said. "There are four more like it, but the other jewellers are in them all day and they lock them when they leave. I wasn't able to catch security taking a washroom break at the same time as one of the jewellers, so I just took shots of my office." While he spoke, he brought up the pictures of his office. David's office was a square that didn't appear to be much bigger than ten-by-ten. There was a desk pushed against the wall in the right corner. On the desk was something that looked like a microscope, a jeweller's monocle, and various tools left wherever they had been put down. All of the equipment surrounded a larger machine in the middle of the desk. The machine had nothing to do with jewellery; at least not the design part. The thirty-second time limit for the slide was up and it was replaced with another image of the room. The new image was from a different angle. The shot showed off a bookcase that was twenty percent full. The spines of the books were just clear enough to make out; all of them were jewellery books. The rest of the bookcase was devoted to housing random items that David had likely brought into his office at one time or another. I saw loose papers, binders, and an empty duffel bag lying unzipped on a shelf. In the half minute of wait time for a new slide, I felt a slight agitation begin to grow in my mind. Something about the slides wasn't sitting right, but I couldn't put my finger on it. I probed my mind, sending sonar out into its depths, but whatever had prodded my brain had dove deep. The image on the television changed again. The new image was of the back of the office door. The door was open and through it I could see down the hall to another door, this one out of focus.

"That door looks different," I said.

David looked at the screen and then back at me with a quizzical expression on his face.

"The one down the hall."

"Oh, that's Saul's office," he said.

"We never saw that," I said.

"That's because no one gets in there without him. Saul makes sure of that."

"You have nothing else on that office?" I asked.

David shook his head. "I was lucky to get that shot of the safe."

"But you've been in there?"

He laughed. "A million times."

"Sketch it out," I said.

"I can do that."

"Now," I said. "We'll wait. In the meantime, run the slideshow again."

"Again?" Johnny said. "We just saw it twice."

"You ready to sign on?"

Johnny shrugged. "Money is right. That's enough for me."

"Enough for me, too," Tony said.

"What other reason do you need?"

"Was the money right on the job that put you inside?"

Johnny's eyes narrowed. "What the fuck you know about that?"

"The ink on your arm says you've been inside."

Johnny looked at his forearm. "So the fuck what?"

"The fuck," I said, "is what I'm asking about. Was it the money that caused the fuck?"

"Nah, it wasn't the money. I got sold out. A guy on our crew got pinched and traded up. I took the fall and kept my mouth shut 'cause I'm a stand-up con."

"And now you're out and looking to start earning again," I said.

"Damn straight. I missed out on seven years of work."

"Seven years away isn't a reason to take a job."

"It ain't just that," Johnny said. "The money is right, and I seen the job. I think we can make it work."

"You've seen the job?" I said.

"Twice."

"How many cameras?"

"What?"

"How many cameras are positioned around the store?"

Johnny looked at the television. The slides were moving too slowly to give him any help.

"David, is there any food left?" I asked.

"Yeah, tons."

I looked at Johnny. "Go get something to eat." When the big man didn't answer, I said it again, "Go get something to eat."

He gave me his version of a hard stare. "Who died and put you in charge?"

Miles cut in. "I got this. My dangerous-guy banter has been getting better." He looked at Johnny. "Okay, say that again, but say it to me, not to Wilson."

Johnny's fists clenched into two flesh-and-bone sledge-hammers. Whatever anger he had worked up for me had just fuelled the forest fire he already had burning for Miles.

"Just get a plate and sit down," I said. "The warm shrimp has to be better than listening to Miles."

Miles looked at me. "That was hurtful."

"I've just about had it with this shit," Johnny said. He started to walk away, but then turned to face me. "You and I aren't done. Not by a fucking mile."

"Doesn't have to be a mile to be done," I said. "It's just ten feet to the food."

I nodded at David. "Again."

The three men on the couch were still seated. Diego #1 said, "You heard the man."

"I've seen this thing more times than I can count," Alvin said. "I'm getting something to eat."

"No one, but that could change."

I looked at Miles. "What?"

"That was the line." He did a terrible impression of Johnny's deep southern drawl. "*Who died and put you in charge? No one, but that could change. Badass right?*"

I ignored him and watched the slides again.

"It was a pretty good line."

Miles looked over at the woman still seated in her chair. "It was wasn't it?"

"Very Eastwood," she said.

The slides shifted from the door to reception.

Miles ignored the TV in favour of the woman. "How'd you get in on this?"

"Every job needs a driver."

"And that's you?"

The woman leaned forward. She had taken off her jacket after the first run through the slides and folded it over her knee. The plaid button-down she wore fell a few inches and exposed the top of her bra. "You have a problem with that?"

"What, because you're a girl? Or because you're black?"

"Take your pick."

"I don't have a thing about girls behind the wheel. And as for the race thing, it's not like you're Chinese."

The woman leaned back and gave Miles a sour look. Her obvious distaste lasted until she noticed Miles laughing at her.

"You're screwing with me."

"Just a little," Miles said. "Now, let me ask you something. As our official driver, what is your policy on rides home?"

The woman held out her middle finger. "You can ride this."

"Got it. There's only room for one."

I looked at Miles. "Shut up."

Miles looked back at the woman. "See why I need a ride home?"

If anyone said anything during the rest of the slideshow, I didn't notice. I couldn't see the job yet; it was there, but I couldn't see it. I knew that if I just kept watching, I would see something in the slides that we could take advantage of. Once I had that, the rest of the job would fall in line. It was there, buried in the images. I just had to keep looking for it. There was something else about the job that I couldn't see yet — something lurking beneath the surface. It had bothered me on the first run through and I was determined to work it out. I used the slides to mentally walk the space. I noticed things I had missed on the other runs, but I didn't find a solution to my two problems. I didn't see the job yet, and I couldn't shake that feeling living in the back of my mind. I stared, lost in thought, at the final image of the safe until the screen went black.

Johnny rested his pool cue against the side of the table and took hold of the two corner pockets. "You ready to sit down about this?"

"I want to see it again."

Johnny threw up his hands. "You got to be fuckin' kiddin' me!"

I ignored the big ex-con and caught David's eye. "Play it again."

David nodded, but I could see that he didn't have much patience left. He hit the keyboard with a hard jab and muttered, "I'm getting something to eat."

The words were petulant, but they seemed to have the power of a burger chain slogan. The Diegos got up and followed David to what was left of the chips.

The computer tech got up a second later and spent a bit of time pulling up his pants. "I'll leave you to it," he said.

"We might as well get something, too," Miles said. "This could take a while." Miles and the woman got up and found a bowl of popcorn in an unoccupied corner of the room.

"Don't listen to them." I turned my head and saw Alvin crouching down so that his mouth was level with my ear. "Take all the time you need."

I spoke without taking my eyes off the screen. "I was going to anyway. I either take the time to look over the job now, or I do the time later."

"You mind telling me what it is you're looking for?"

"The job," I said.

"You aren't going to find a better one. At least not one that pays like this."

"I don't doubt that the money is there. I can see that. What I can't see is how to walk away with it."

"You saying it can't be done?"

"I'm saying I can't see it — yet."

Alvin was quiet for the next few slides. When he finally spoke again, it was quiet. "When I reached out to Jake about this job, I asked him to put in a call to you. I wanted you on this."

I said nothing.

"You put together a job for me about a year back."

"I remember. It was a three-man takedown of a

high-roller card game." Alvin had worked out the, 'Freeze, nobody move!' all on his own. He was just lacking the how to get in and, more importantly, how to get away. I had been working as a set-up man for a while using Jake as my broker. Jake was a professional middleman for crooks. For a finder's fee, Jake offered to connect people with reliable professionals. Alvin got in touch with Jake and he, after he had collected his money, gave Alvin a way to get in touch with me. Alvin told me about the score; I got five grand for figuring out how he would get it and keep it. "How much was the take?"

"A hundred split three ways."

"Makes all that time arguing about spending five on me seem reasonable."

Alvin put his hands up. "I'm man enough to admit when I'm wrong. That's why I asked Jake to get a line out to you. You got us in and out of that game without a hitch. We need that here."

"That's the problem," I said. "All I see here are diamonds and hitches."

Miles spoke up from the other side of the room. "Sounds like a country song."

Alvin ignored Miles. "Keep looking. There has to be a way." He laughed to himself. "You know how many people I told about that card job? No one believes the part about the fire hydrant. If you figured that out, you'll get this."

"Is that what this is about?" Johnny called from the pool table.

Miles had worked his way into a game and had been about to break when Johnny bellowed. He looked up at the bigger man with a scowl on his face. Johnny liked that; he liked it so much he waited for the cue to move again before he finished his thought. "You need a way in? I got your way in. Just ask nicely with a big fucking gun."

I ignored the con. The slides kept to their leisurely pace. After ten of them, I tilted my head and spoke to Alvin without taking my eyes off the screen. "Why are you here, Alvin?"

"I tol' you, Wilson. It's Vin."

"Tell me why you're here. Are you here for you or are you here for your brother-in-law?"

Alvin smiled. "A little from column A; a little from column B. The take from the card game didn't last as long as I had hoped it would. I bought a few things. Low-key shit. A leather jacket, a couple rounds, a motorcycle."

"Low key," I said.

"Anyway, a guy from the neighbourhood ratted me out to another guy from the neighbourhood. Guy number two was someone I owed some money to. And before you know it, poof, thirty becomes zero. Well, negative three thousand. All because of a goddamn rat."

"What did you say?"

"Negative three thousand. I had ten left, but I owed thirteen."

"No," I said. "Not that. The guy from the neighbourhood."

"The rat?"

"The rat," I said. I sat back and took my eyes off the screen. I didn't need to watch anymore. I had found what I was looking for, and my mind was busy running with it. "You can turn that off. I'm ready."

CHAPTER THREE

We were all sitting down around the coffee table. The computer had been pushed back and the television was off. There was a clock on the wall with its hands competing for the twelve.

"Alright," Alvin said. "You've all seen the job. And you all stayed, so that means you want in. Now, we talk details."

David leaned forward, positioned his hands like a director framing a movie scene, and took over. "I figure you should hit the store in the daytime when everyone is busy working. You could round everyone up, lock the doors, and then use the rest of the day to get into the safes. You just need to come up with a way to deal with the security system."

No one said anything.

"It's a good plan," David said.

"It's a bad movie," I said.

"*Reservoir Dogs*," Miles said.

"You're not hearing me," David said. "You could lock up the place and cancel all of the appointments. You'd have all day."

"Front to back is a linear progression," I said. "Won't work."

"What the hell does that even mean?" Johnny said.

I looked at the bigger man. "It means front to back is a straight line with two locked doors and three cameras before we even get to the showroom. We'll be watched the whole way, and the second any of us get out of line, the guard watching the cameras is going to hit the alarm."

"But we can hack the alarm and make it so it doesn't work," David said. His tone was becoming condescending.

"So the alarm doesn't work. Where does that get us?"

"It gets you inside," David said.

I nodded. "With two guns in front of us and eight cell phones. Have you watched the news lately? They don't even need cameramen anymore; everyone is a goddamn breaking-news reporter. An alarm is easier to deal with than the people."

"So what do we do?" David asked.

"We do it at night. You said Saul leaves around eight and doesn't come back until nine the next day. Night means more than twelve hours with no people and no cell phones to deal with. We just need to get around the alarm."

David cut in, "Can you do that, Elliot? Can you get in?"

"You mean hack the panel and get us in?"

"Yeah."

"It could be done," Elliot said as he cleaned his glasses with the bottom of his shirt. "But it wouldn't do you any good."

"What do you mean?"

"The easiest way in is to rig the machine to register a

legitimate entry. I saw the alarm panel in the pictures. The image is enough for me to get the specs."

"So what's the problem?"

"The problem is an after-hours entry will show up on the alarm company's computer. Judging from the outside panel, the system is expensive. That means the company running it is all about bells and whistles. An after-hours entry, legitimate or not, is going to warrant some attention. Most likely, the security company will turn on the cameras and take a look."

"So let's give them something to look at," Miles said.

"Like what?" Elliot countered.

"Like David," Miles said.

"What? That's not part of the plan. I'm just the inside man."

"Relax," Miles said. "No one is asking you to hold a gun or anything. You just need to walk in, go to your office to get something you forgot, and then set the alarm again when you leave."

"How does that help us?" Elliot asked.

"If there is a blind spot, we can get to it while the alarm is powered down. Then David seals us inside with the alarm back on."

"Two problems," David said. "One, I seriously doubt there's a blind spot, and two, I don't have the alarm code."

"That's a possible problem and a technicality," Miles said. "We could solve problem number one by manufacturing a blind spot."

Johnny elbowed his partner. "Listen to this asshole. How the hell do you manufacture a blind spot?"

The room went quiet and all eyes were on Miles. "Off the top of my head, I'd say a spotlight through the doorway would blind the camera and get us inside to a place that's out of frame."

The answer was interesting — really interesting. It shut Johnny up and everyone else waited for Miles to go on.

"Problem number two is no problem at all. No one knows you don't have an access code. Who's to say your boss didn't give you the code during one of his episodes? If the security company turns on the cameras and you're doing something mundane like grabbing your coat, what are they going to do? You think they'll call the cops?"

"We don't know what they'll do," Elliot said.

"So we do a dry run. David will be our canary in a diamond mine. We send him in and see what happens. If it works out, the next time we send him in, he won't be alone."

"I don't know if I like it," David said. "It's a lot of risk."

"There's some of that when you decide to steal millions from your boss."

"It's not a bad plan," Elliot said.

"Thank you," Miles said.

"There are some strong elements to it, but it won't work here."

"Wait. What?" Miles said. "Why not?"

I looked at Elliot. "Tell him."

"Tell me what?"

"Your whole plan hinges on sneaking us in and stashing us until the cameras stop watching," Elliot said.

"Right," Miles said.

"But that isn't an option — not with those motion sensors."

"Motion sensors?" David said.

"On the underside of the camera," Elliot said. "You can see the lens if you know where to look."

"Even if there was a blind spot, the cameras would pick us up the second we left it."

"Well, fuck," Miles said.

"So we're back to square one," David said.

"What do we need?" I said.

"Diamonds," Diego #2 said. "We need diamonds."

I nodded. "And what do we need to do to get them?"

"We need to get inside without setting off the alarms," Diego #1 said.

I looked at Elliot. "Can you do that?"

"I can do that, but not from the front door. I'd need a crack at the computers in that back office."

"You ever do something like that before?" Alvin asked.

"Sort of. Not in a jewellery store."

"But you think you can?" David said.

Elliot nodded. "Back in school, I rigged a security system to do something similar. We walked into the Dean's office and stole all of his furniture without a single alarm sounding."

There was a short silence while everyone appraised Elliot. The man was in no kind of shape. His body was slowly deflating, and he wasn't working on keeping the sinking ship clean. His hair was greasy; his glasses were greasier. The slovenly appearance made his age difficult to determine.

"School?" Johnny said. "You did something like this in school? I stole a kid's lunch money when I was in school; I threatened to stab him with a plastic fork from the cafeteria unless he gave up his allowance. I guess to you that would count as successful armed robbery experience."

Elliot fixed his four eyes on Johnny. "The school was MIT, so no."

"So you're good," Miles said.

Elliot nodded. "I don't think I would be here if I wasn't."

"You get away with it?" I asked.

Elliot shook his head.

"Not so good," Miles said.

Elliot pushed his glasses up his nose. "The work wasn't the issue. The work was top-notch hacking. I didn't get caught because I was sloppy; I got caught because my roommate walked in on me when I was writing the worm. It was the damnest thing. He was eating a burrito and it squirted onto his shirt. He went over to my console because I kept Kleenex next to my computer —"

Miles snickered.

"You never peak at someone's screen. It's an unwritten rule. But when he grabbed the Kleenex, he saw it. It was right in front of his face. When word about the Dean's office got out, he turned me in. He hated my guts because he thought I hacked his Warcraft account. I did, but he couldn't prove it. That pissed him off even more than the hack. So when he had something he could prove, he did."

"Back to good then," Miles said.

"I can co-opt the system, but I need to get into it. For what is at stake, I'd need to do the work on-site."

"How do we make that happen?" David said.

"Not my department," Elliot said.

"You can't do it using the internet or something?" Johnny said. "We'll make sure no one walks in eating a burrito." He looked at Diego #1. "Right?"

Diego #1 gave Johnny a look that was all ice. "I'm not that guy. You try that shit and it will go somewhere. Comprende?"

Johnny smiled. "I like this one."

"Johnny makes a point. You sure you can't hack the system remotely?" David asked.

"This isn't a registrar's office," Elliot said. "The system in place is expensive, and expensive means good. I can't just sit at a Starbucks around the corner and take control of the store with my laptop. I need access to the site so I can introduce a virus that will get us what we need."

"So we have a man who can turn off the alarm and cameras provided we get him in so he can look over the computers," I said.

"And how do we do that?" David asked.

"We don't," I said. "You do."

CHAPTER FOUR

"This again? I'm the inside man. I'm not supposed to be a part of the robbery. That wasn't part of the plan."

"There never was a plan," I said, "just a goal."

"My goal was to stay out of it."

I shook my head. "Not possible. You have a part to play in this and the sooner you get your head around it, the sooner we will have a plan. You said that Saul planned on handing over the business to you one day."

David leaned forward in his chair and brought his hands together. "That was always the plan."

"Does that mean he considers you important?"

"Of course."

"He relies on you?"

David rotated his wedding band again and again. "Yes."

"You're the number two in the operation?"

"Yes." David put a little edge on the word. Things were getting away from him, and he didn't like it.

"If the toilet breaks, what happens?"

He took his hand off his ring. "What?"

"Yeah, what?" Johnny said.

"Just tell me what happens if the toilet breaks," I said.

"Where are you going with this?" Diego #1 asked.

"Let's hear him out," Alvin said.

"If it breaks, who handles it? You? Saul? Someone else?"

"I do."

"What about a problem with the register. Who takes care of that?"

"Me," David said.

"A computer issue?"

David's eyes opened wide. "Me. I do. I think I see where this is going. You want me to make a call to a computer repairman, and that repairman will be Elliot."

I nodded. "But first, I want you to break the computer."

CHAPTER FIVE

"**I** can't break the computer."

"Sure you can," I said. "You just need to do exactly what I tell you to do."

"I keep telling you, me being involved was never part of the plan."

"Having us over to your house to eat warm shrimp in your rumpus room —"

"Thank you," Miles said.

"— so we can look at pictures *you* took of where *you* work — so that *we* could rob it — makes *you* involved."

Alvin nodded. "He's right, David. You're the inside man."

"And that means we need you to get inside," I said.

"That's why they don't call it the outside man," Miles said. He looked around the room. "Am I right?" He got four eye rolls and no responses.

"You're the only way this works," I said.

Johnny looked like he was gearing up to say something, but David spoke first. "So how do I break a computer that belongs to a guy who sits in front of it all day. It's not like I can just wait for him to take a piss. If he leaves his office and comes back to find his station wrecked, he's going to know something is up. The first thing he'll do once that computer is back up and running is check the tapes. When that happens, I'm fucked. We are all fucked. You ever consider that? Or are you going to tell me that is part of the plan, too?"

"What was that?" Johnny said. "You want to say that again?"

If David realized what he had just said, it wasn't written on his face. His brother-in-law, however, did get it; Alvin looked down and began kneading his eyes with his thumb and index finger.

Johnny stood up. "Say that again."

Alvin lifted an agitated face out of his hand. "He didn't mean it that way. Tell 'em, Dave. Tell 'em you didn't mean it that way." The words came out casual, but Alvin's eyes were all business.

"What?"

Alvin sighed. "That if *you're* fucked, it doesn't mean that *we're* fucked."

"What?" After several long seconds, David understood his error. "Oh, no. No. No, I didn't mean it like that."

"You sure?" Johnny asked.

"Yeah, I just meant the job would be finished is all. That's what would be fucked. I mean, I couldn't do anything to you guys if I wanted to. All I know is your first names. And, that's if they even are your first names."

I stopped David while he was just barely ahead. "I don't even want you to do anything conspicuous. In fact, I need you to do the opposite. I just need you to get inside that office a couple of times."

David sighed. "What do you want me to do?"

I told him.

"No. No way. No fucking way. Are you kidding? I'll get sick or something. Those things carry all kinds of diseases. Who knows what I'll get."

"They were responsible for the bubonic plague," Miles said.

"You hear that? Fucking plague. That's what I'm going to get. The plague."

"We'll get clean ones," I lied. "They sell them at the pet store."

"I don't know," he said.

"You'll only need to get in a couple of times. The *night shift* will take care of the rest. Then when the computers stop working, you make sure that you are the one to make the call."

"Crazy as it sounds, it makes sense," Diego #1 said. "If it works, it will get us inside for the entire night without the cameras or the security company to worry about. It's a good plan."

"Says the guy who doesn't have to walk around with a rat strapped to his thigh."

"Not your thigh," I said. I pointed towards David's pants. "There's not enough room for what you're going to carry. It will need to go in the crotch."

David's eyes bulged. "You've got to be fucking kidding me."

I shook my head. "We'll need to have a specialized cage

made up. I'll talk to some people. We also need to think about the windows."

"Windows? Why does the rat need to see my dick?"

"No, the store windows. We have the cameras covered, but there is still the guard outside to consider." I looked at the Diegos. "We're going to need to have the lights on."

"Can't do something like this in the dark," Diego #2 said.

"Can't rule out a torch either," added his brother.

"We can use tarps," Johnny said. "We can just duct tape them to the wall. We'll just need the window measurements to make sure we get 'em big enough."

"And how do I explain why I'm measuring the windows?"

"We'll use spray paint," I said. "Less to measure and less to carry."

"You got a clever answer for everything, don't you?"

"I better," I said. "No one pays for the other kind."

"So it looks like you're telling everyone what to do. You're the man with the plan, David is a walking catch and release, the jumping beans are on the boxes, and Elliot is the geek squad. What about the rest of us, *boss*?" Coming from Johnny, the word boss had an unhealthy dose of sarcasm added to it.

I looked at Johnny. "You, Tony, and Alvin are inside with me. We'll be sealing up the place and taking orders from the Diegos."

"So we're the hired help. That it?"

"We have ten men for a five-man job," I said. "That was the hand we were dealt. I'm just playing it."

I looked over at the woman beside Miles. "No offence."

She smiled. "Doesn't bother me if you want to call him a man."

Johnny looked at the woman. "What the fuck did you just say to me?"

Alvin put up two palms. "C'mon, Johnny, we're not here for this."

"He's right," I said.

"Is he? You deciding that, too? Alright, boss, why don't you tell me what the bitch and the mouth are doing."

"Bitch? Which one of us do you think he means?" Miles said.

The woman narrowed her eyes. "He means you," she said.

Johnny laughed. "That mean you want to be the mouth?"

"They're in the car," I said.

"Them?"

I nodded.

"You got me inside taking orders and them in the car."

I nodded again. "Alvin found her the same way he found me — through Jake. That means she's good behind the wheel."

It was true. No one got on Jake's Rolodex without being reliable. I could see where Johnny's mind was on the issue; I could see it, but I didn't share his view.

Whatever the bigger man's opinion of the opposite sex, gender didn't have a place in this argument. Physically, there was nothing a man could do behind the wheel that a woman couldn't duplicate. There were, in fact, distinct advantages to using a woman on the job instead of a man

— underestimated people have distinct advantages.

"She's the driver," I said. "She's in the car."

"She has a name."

I looked at the driver.

"Monica," she said.

I looked back at Johnny. "Monica is the wheelman."

Johnny jabbed a thick finger towards Miles. "And why him?"

"He's our con man."

"Why the fuck do we need one of those in the car? Why do we need one of those period?"

"Monica is going to follow the security guard on his route for the night. If she gets made, Miles is going to talk their way out of it."

Johnny laughed out loud and Tony joined in. "This annoying fuck is going to talk his way out of a jam? He's been here a couple of hours and the fact that he's standing is a miracle."

I nodded. "He's been riding you?"

"He's been annoying the shit out of me."

"I bet you've been dying to shut him up."

"You have no idea."

"Who suggested the game?"

"What?"

"You were playing pool with Miles. Whose idea was it to play? Doesn't matter, you likely feel it was yours."

Johnny looked at Miles, but he wasn't there anymore; at least, not the same Miles who had walked in the door a couple of hours ago. The loud, obnoxious asshole had been replaced with someone different. This version of

Miles leaned back in his chair with an air of cool that Paul Newman would have had trouble duplicating. Miles lifted an eyebrow at Johnny and shrugged. When he met my eye, the calm demeanour faltered for a split second. I saw something — something angry — play across his face, but only for a second.

I didn't wait for an answer to my question; instead, I posed another, "How much on the game?"

"Ten thousand," Johnny said.

I looked at Miles. If the anger was still there, I couldn't detect it. What I could detect was the scam. "But we're not talking about cash are we? No, this is ten thousand after the job is over, right?"

Johnny wore an expression of confusion; when he saw my grin, it turned to anger. Money you haven't made yet is far easier to spend than what's in your pocket. Las Vegas figured that out a million years ago. Give someone a stack of cash and they'll guard it with their lives when they figure out it's leaking away. Give them a stack of colourful chips and they'll give them the same attention they give their reading glasses. The value of money is relative to proximity; Miles knows that. That was why it would have never been just ten. Ten would have become twenty in about half the time it would take for it to become forty.

Johnny began to catch up. "You son of a bitch."

Miles eased out of his recline and subtly put his hands on his knees. "I think a fight would ruin this fine rumpus room. Why don't we just call it a draw and get another beer."

Johnny stood.

Rather than get up, Miles put a foot on the coffee table. It was smart; it was what I would have done. I told Johnny to sit down before Miles decided to kick the table forward into the bigger man's knees. Eventually, after he completed what he must have felt was the appropriate amount of alpha-male stare down, Johnny sat down.

We sat around the table for another two hours, laying out the job and logging what needed to be done. In three weeks, we'd do the job.

CHAPTER SIX

The next morning, I woke at six and used the cramped floor space of the hotel room to grind through a workout. An hour later, I was showered, dressed, and ready for breakfast. I checked out and slid behind the wheel of the rental car. The hotel was one of dozens surrounding LaGuardia, and I planned to make use of more than one of them. I had three weeks until the job, and I was going to use the hotels to play a shell game. It wasn't paranoia; I didn't think there were people out there who wanted to kill me — I knew it. I wasn't concerned about the men I had met the night before, but I didn't write them off, either. Experience had taught me to think moves ahead of anyone on the other side of the board and to expect that there was always someone playing against me. The only payout guaranteed to a professional thief is enemies, and I had earned well. My head didn't rest easier on a new pillow each night. I didn't fear for my life; I just had zero desire to make the act of killing me easier on anyone. If someone wanted to punch my ticket, they had to put in the goddamn legwork or go the fuck home.

I stopped at a diner and ate amongst the herd of weary travellers who were either just getting in or just about to leave. I finished my plate and got on the road. Traffic was heavy for anywhere in the world that wasn't New York, but that didn't matter — I had planned for it. I got to the jewellery store an hour before it was set to open and found every space on the street occupied. I parked in a lot and paid enough to bribe a crooked politician for a parking space and worked my way back on foot. I found a seat in a coffee shop with a view of Mendelson's Jewellery and set up shop with a coffee, muffin, and a newspaper. I ignored everything but my drink while I watched the store. The building was a rare two-storey on the outskirts of the diamond district. The brick exterior was aged, but the well-maintained masonry held on to the kind of deep red usually reserved for Rockwell paintings. The windows were thick and tall. David had said the building had once been two separate stories, but after Saul hit the big time, he bought out the second floor and created a single-floor building with impossibly high ceilings. Saul must have paid a fortune to window washers; the dark-tinted glass was immaculately clean and reflected an incredibly intense amount of sunlight across the street and into my eyes.

I was nursing my second cup of coffee when a man turned from the sidewalk and went up the stairs. He was young; thirty was probably still in the rear-view. The Sudan had imparted its unique imprint on the man's skin and, from the looks of his fur-lined hat, had not prepared him for the cold winter climate of New York. In David's basement, I had seen multiple images of the man. He was one of the store's two security guards. The guard did something interesting; he stayed on the steps. Instead of going into the store, he just stood around with his hands deep inside his jacket pockets. I watched his breath fog the air as I sipped my cold cup of coffee. He waited, shivering, for five minutes for the boss to show. Saul approached the door on foot from the direction of Ninth Avenue. David had told us that Saul had a parking space up the street in a private lot, but he neglected to get shots of it. Saul had owned the spot for nearly two decades and apparently loved to brag about it.

Saul walked with stooped shoulders and a creased brow. If he ever did decide to retire, he could easily find seasonal work playing Ebenezer Scrooge. When Saul got to the top of the stairs, the security guard stepped down. Saul checked over his shoulder to make sure the guard was not able to see the alarm pad and then punched in the code. He walked inside without holding the door open for his employee. The guard jogged up the steps and caught the door without any sign of surprise — it was routine. I watched him enter behind his boss and immediately close the door behind him. A minute or so later, lights turned on in the windows. I reflected on the entry and wondered if there was a way to spin it. If the entry was a routine repeated every day, there might be a way to brace both men at the door and get inside. Once inside, we could just wait for everyone else to show and round them up as they walked through the door. The idea was raw, and I picked at it while I watched the door from my seat. Three minutes later, another man in pants that matched the first security guard jogged up to the door. He was a midfifties Latino in dark pants and cop shoes. Even if David hadn't described him, I would have pegged the ex-cop as security. The second guard waited only seconds before he was buzzed in. The speed told me that the other guard was already in his office and on the cameras. Four more employees showed up within ten minutes of the other guard and were admitted with the same efficiency. The whole operation ran exactly the way David said it would, with one exception: David wasn't there.

CHAPTER SEVEN

I ordered a third coffee and watched the jewellery store some more. No one went in and no one came out. Once the coffee lost all of its warmth, I got off my chair and left the shop. It was closing in on lunchtime, and I wanted to see why David wasn't at work.

David was certainly no pro, but he must have had enough sense to realize that to avoid being pegged as the inside man, he had to avoid looking like the inside man. The entire job hinged on the access he could get us, and that access had the potential to diminish with every mistake he made. I needed to find him and make him understand that from now until the day of the job, David had to be employee of the month.

The traffic into Jersey City was thick, but I made it there in just over an hour. Any ideas I had about available midday parking spaces vanished as I passed David's house. Every spot near his place was taken; even the driveway was full. The two-car driveway had three cars artfully crammed into it, making use of the grass and flirting with the curb. None of the cars was the Volkswagen David had been driving.

I parked on a side street and walked past the townhouse. Through the windows, I could see people moving around, but I couldn't make out if any of them was David. It was a residential street, so there was no place to stake out the house where I wouldn't bring attention to myself. I had no choice but to keep moving. I worked small circuits around David's house, careful to keep my head moving back and forth; if anyone asked, I'd just say that I was looking for a lost dog.

On my eighth pass by the front door, I finally caught someone leaving the house. The man was old and out of shape. His puffy, aged skin had the lumpy look of hastily shaped clay. He fumbled with the zipper of his jacket as he hustled down the stairs, a cigarette dangling from his thick lips. He went to the rearmost car and rummaged around in the front seat until he found a lighter. I slowed my pace and let my face soften. When I spoke, my voice came out higher and less threatening.

"You haven't seen a dog have you? He's a little guy. A Yorkie."

The old guy finished lighting his cigarette and waited until he had pulled in a lungful of smoke before he answered.

"Just got out here."

"Shit," I said. "It's my girlfriend's dog. I took her out for a pee and she bolted on me. I have to find her before my girlfriend gets back from work or I'll never hear the end of it."

The old guy was concentrating on the cigarette more than on me. He took another drag and took his time letting it out before he replied. "Sorry, can't help you."

"Dave wouldn't be around, would he? If he's got some time, I could use the help."

The old guy was no longer interested in the cigarette. He looked at me with an expression that was hard to read. I couldn't tell if he was angry or sad. An uncomfortable silence hung in the air with his secondhand smoke.

"Something I said?"

The old guy dropped his cigarette and ground it out with one slow twist of his shoe. "You and David close?"

"We get a drink every now and again," I said. "We're both in the same line of work. Is he around?"

The old guy shook his head. "I'm really sorry to tell you this, but David died last night."

"Died?"

"He and his brother-in-law were killed in a car accident. They were out late and they had been drinking. The police found bottles in the car with them. Anyway, they went off the road and into a ravine."

"Alvin was in the car?"

The old guy nodded. "You knew Alvin, too?"

I nodded. "I met him through David. He was a good guy."

"David was my nephew on my wife's side. The whole family is devastated. Just devastated."

"You have my condolences," I said. "You and your family."

"Thank you."

I nodded and walked back towards the car. Our inside man was gone and the job was dead.

CHAPTER EIGHT

I called Jake as I drove out of Jersey.

"Tommy's Super Fantastic Funporium," a chipper voice answered.

"I'd like to speak with Jake."

"I'm sorry, sir," the woman on the other end said in a voice so enthusiastic that it had to be an act. "He isn't here right now. Could I connect you with his voicemail?"

"Perfect," I said.

The line went quiet and then I heard Jake's deep baritone. "You've reached Jake McKean, owner of Tommy's Super Fantastic Funporium. I am away from my desk at the moment, but if you leave your name, phone number, and a brief message, I will return your call at my earliest convenience. Have a super fantastic day."

When the machine beeped, I left a short message; ten words to be exact. I hung up the phone and changed lanes to avoid getting trapped behind a tractor-trailer.

Jake returned my message a half hour later. I picked up on the first ring. I wasn't anxious; there was just nothing else to do while I was trapped in bumper-to-bumper traffic.

"I'm returning a call on my voicemail," Jake said.

"Is this a clean line?"

"I'm on my cell if that's what you mean." It was.

"The job is off," I said.

"I'm sorry. You're going to have to be more specific."

"David and Alvin are dead."

Jake sighed. "That is specific. Was it a difference in opinion?"

He wanted to know if I had killed them. "Car accident."

"That doesn't answer my question."

"I don't know if the car had an opinion," I said.

"What do you need from me?"

"Nothing. This was a courtesy call."

"You leaving town?"

I let the question hang for a second before I said, "Yes."

"I'll let you know if anything else pops up."

"You might want to reach out to the others and give them the news."

"I can do that."

I ended the call and kept driving. Jake was a fitter. He connected management and labour. If you had a job you wanted to pull, Jake had connections to a network of pros who could do it. I had first connected with Jake after I pulled a score in Vegas and moved the profits to Glen, a moneyman in Oklahoma. Glen worked off of a Native reserve and washed money through the local casino. He was funnelling the clean money into investments that generated income and were as legal as a McDonald's.

I had called Glen after I hit the interstate. Vegas was in my rear-view, but the money was still in the trunk. He answered the phone right away. "I thought you were dead."

Glen had written me off because I had been off the grid — some bad business in Buffalo had taken me out of the game for a little while. "Not yet."

"You get pinched?"

"No."

"Well, you're still as chatty as ever."

"I have business."

"You don't need to be chatty when you've got money. How much we talking about."

"Twenty-five."

"That it? I wish you had gotten pinched. There's more money in prison."

"I've been moving around."

"That shouldn't be a problem if you know the right people," Glen had said.

"Too many people know the people I know."

"They don't know the people I know."

It was true. Glen was good at what he did and that meant he dealt with a lot of people who were also good at what they did. He got in touch with Jake, and a week later I had a job lined up. Jake was a professional; his jobs paid well and there was no shortage of work. Knowing better than to shit where I ate, I set up shop outside of New York and flew in whenever I had business.

I had told Jake that I was leaving, and I planned to; I just had a stop to make first.

CHAPTER NINE

It was cold outside and the sun had set early. I was in a heavy peacoat and a knit hat, watching Saul defy a conception I held about the elderly. Every old person I had ever met was always cold. It didn't matter what month it was; if you were in the final season of your life, it was cold. Standing on the street corner with a view of the jewellery store, I watched Saul Mendelson walk on the opposite side of the street with his jacket open. I let him pass me and get a long lead before I followed after him. Saul strode down the street with purpose and a vulture's posture. His pace was interrupted twice by the outstretched hands belonging to bundled men nesting on the pavement. Both times, he slowed and reached into his coat before he arced around the vagrant. The dip of the old man's hand into his coat gave the men a moment of hope, but the hand never came back with money; it lingered inside the jacket until the jeweller was twenty feet away. There was no doubt the old jeweller was carrying.

Saul walked to a parking structure and left in a glossy BMW. I watched the car glide down the street and out of sight before I turned back and walked the way I had come. I found a window seat in the same overpriced café and watched the jewellery store while I let the coffee warm me from the inside out. The security company's car made its first pass a half hour later. The next lap came fifteen minutes after that. I sat for two more laps that came within minutes of duplicating the previous circuit and then walked back to my car. Overall, David had been accurate about the details; it made me think he had been accurate about the money, too.

I had told Jake that the job was off, and I wasn't lying. The job, as it stood, was off. David and Alvin had set up a score and they were gone; their score went with them. More accurately, *their* score went with them, not *the* score.

The next day, I was back for the store's open and close. I had coffee again, but I wasn't outside this time. I had picked up a white panel van from a dealership the day before. The van had clearly been a lot of people's white panel van before it was mine, but I didn't care; I only needed it to stay in place and blend in. I didn't haggle for the van. I bought it for more cash than the dealer asked for, but he had to throw in no questions about it. I had bought a Thermos after I drove the van off the lot, and I filled it at four a.m., just before I went trolling for a parking spot. I had managed to park on a side street in a spot that offered a distant view of the wide front door of Mendelson's Jewellery. With the binoculars I picked up when I bought the Thermos, I could sit out of sight and just barely make out the numbers above the door. On schedule, Saul approached the store from the direction of the parking garage; both security guards were already on the steps waiting to be let inside. When Saul met them, he had words for the younger guard, who had been late the day before. The guard nodded emphatically and then he and his partner stepped down so that Saul could key in the entry code. The three men entered, and minutes later, the other employees began to arrive. The end of the night followed the same methodical rhythm of the morning routine. Employees left the store until Saul, flanked by the two security guards, walked out the door.

Saul's entry and exit on day three and four were carbon copies of day number two. On day five, there was a change; no one showed up on day five. Day five was David's funeral, and Saul had given everyone the day off to attend. I watched the funeral from a distance and waited for something to stand out. Nothing gave me pause. Everyone came, everyone cried, everyone went home. I was back on day six waiting for a re-run of the first three days, but I didn't get it.

Saul was on time. Every one of his arrivals that I had witnessed occurred within five minutes of each other, and day six was no exception. He walked down the street with purpose, ignoring any smile pointed his way. His momentum evaporated when he got close enough to see the front door. Unlike the other days, there was no one waiting. On day one, only one of the guards had been there, and that was enough for Saul to blow a gasket. On the days that followed, there were two men waiting for the jeweller and, judging from the face of the younger guard when Saul had dressed him down, that was the way it was supposed to be.

The old man slowed and then stopped. His body became an obstacle that people scrambled to pass to avoid colliding with his static frame. The old man was oblivious to the dirty looks that were being hurled at him; he was focused on something else. His long vulture neck swung his head in every conceivable direction. Nowhere he looked had what he was searching for. Saul worked his way through three hundred sixty degrees and then crossed the street towards the coffee shop. He cut through a gap in the morning traffic, expecting the drivers to avoid him rather than the opposite. Before he touched the other side of the street, he had a phone to his ear.

When the Sudanese security guard arrived a few minutes later, he was out of breath. He jogged up the steps and breathed a heavy sigh that plumed in the cold morning air. Behind him, the Latino guard strolled up the sidewalk. When the two men met on the steps, they began to argue. There was a lot of pointing from the younger man. The older guard spoke with animated facial expressions and gestures that seemed to enrage his co-worker. The fight ended when the Sudanese man turned his back on the other man. He threw up a hand when the Latino spoke again — he was done talking. The younger man rested his elbows on the railing and leaned over to breathe deeply and catch the breath that didn't have the chance to come back during the argument. After a few long exhalations, he stood and I saw his face. He looked relieved. That all changed when Saul, who had been watching from the same window I had used a few days before, crossed the street and began to scream.

Saul berated the two men on the sidewalk and kept it up as he stomped up the stairs. The younger guard said something and pointed at his partner. Whatever words he had used had been good enough to immediately shift

Saul's focus to the older man. Saul gesticulated wildly as he dressed the retiree down. There was no backtalk this time; the guard just nodded and spoke short responses with his eyes on his shoes. Saul sent the two men down the stairs and then let himself in. The younger guard barely got to the door before it shut in his face.

That evening, Saul walked out with the two guards at his heels. The Sudanese guard held an envelope that he turned over to Saul at the bottom of the stairs. The two men exchanged a few words with each other and then set off in different directions, leaving the second guard to trail his partner.

The next morning, Saul walked up the steps to find his two guards waiting for him. Both men had been early. The Sudanese guard had arrived first; the Latino guard never showed. Instead, a paunchy Asian man in his forties had joined the cameraman. The new triumvirate carried on where the old grouping had left off. I, the silent fourth wheel, kept watching.

The next day, I ate dinner at Tommy's Super Fantastic Funporium.

CHAPTER TEN

Tommy's Super Fantastic Funporium is the answer to the question: how many lights are too many? The building glows — actually glows. The light cast into the sky above Williamsburg can be seen for miles. There was an apartment complex four blocks away that once tried to sue the Funporium because one side of the building thought it diminished the value of their west-facing units. I parked the car and walked through a crowd of smokers fumigating the pavement outside the bar. The interior of the building responded to the light outside as though it were some kind of challenge. The wattage inside Tommy's Super Fantastic Funporium dwarfed the outside. The employees all wore sunglasses during their shifts and it had nothing to do with looking cool.

A young girl in a tie-dye shirt and short-shorts asked me if I was meeting a group or if my friends had already arrived.

"I just want to have a drink at the bar," I said.

The girl gave me a strange look. No one came to the

Funporium to drink alone at the bar. She must have decided that she didn't care enough to ask me about it because she shrugged a response and peeled off a long string of tickets for me. "Make sure to stop by the arcade. We have twenty kinds of pinball, tons of arcade games, and the state's biggest skee-ball machine."

I thanked her and found a spot at the bar. I ordered a beer and kept my hand on the ten that I placed on the counter. When the bartender came to collect, I held on to the bill.

"Jake around?"

"Sorry?" The music was blaring something that was current enough to spur moments of spontaneous dancing from various people in the bar.

"Jake," I yelled.

"He's in his office."

"Where is his office?"

The bartender looked at my hand and the bill underneath.

I walked away from the beer and the bill and headed towards Jake's office next to the kitchen. The door, marked private, was exactly where the bartender said it would be. I turned the knob without knocking and walked in to find Jake getting a backrub from one of the tie-dyed waitresses. The bartender hadn't said anything about this. The girl was older than the other waitresses I had seen but still young enough to be called a girl. She was pretty, but I saw some wear and tear. I guessed the increased mileage meant she had to pay a few tolls to keep working.

"Can't you read? The door was marked —" Jake stopped talking when he saw my face. He sat up a little straighter in his chair, and the girl rubbing his neck noticed a change in the flesh she was working. Her hands slowed down as she tried to get her head around what was happening.

I took a seat in one of the chairs opposite Jake's desk and waited.

"Alison, could you give us a few minutes?"

The waitress bit her lower lip and reluctantly said, "Sure, Jake."

Jake watched her leave and shut the door. When he looked back at me, he said, "It's not what you think."

"What do I think?"

"That I'm some lech who makes the girls sit on my lap for a job."

"She wasn't on your lap," I said.

"No, she was rubbing my back, but not because I made her. I pulled a muscle the other day playing skee-ball and Alison was rubbing my back because she's in school to be a masseuse, or whatever they call that shit these days."

"So she was practicing."

"Yeah."

"Sure."

"You don't believe me? I'm not lying. I really pulled a muscle."

"Okay."

"I'm serious."

"I'm not here to apply for a job, Jake. I don't care what you do with the girls in your office."

"I don't do anything."

I sighed. "I don't care who touches you. I care about who you can touch."

"How many times do I gotta say it? I don't touch the girls."

"Not the girls," I said. "I'm talking about the people you can get in touch with."

"This a work thing?"

"I'm not here to play skee-ball."

Jake rubbed his shoulder. "You shouldn't be. It's dangerous." He leaned back in his chair. "I thought the job was done."

"That job was."

"But you want to resuscitate it."

"You got a nurse rubbing your legs?"

"What?"

"Resuscitate."

"Fuck you, I know what resuscitate means. So you're bringing the job back from the dead?"

"Not that job."

"So this is a new thing."

I nodded. "With some of the old parts."

"Like the score."

"And a few of the players."

"Just a few?" he wanted to know.

"There was a lot of dead weight on the last job."

"You being funny?"

"No."

"'Cause I was friends with Vin."

I stared at Jake and waited to see if the threat would bloom into something with thorns. It didn't.

"Some of those other guys might not like the idea of you cutting them out."

"You going to tell them?"

Jake's eyes widened and he showed me two palms. "Me? You know that's not how I operate. I'm a fitter."

"Then stop trying to give me advice."

"Fine, fine. Jesus, you are a bastard. What do you need?"

"I need you to get word out to two of the original crew."

"Vin asked for eight bodies."

"That's right."

"But you want two."

"Yes."

Jake stared at me like he wanted to ask more questions. I didn't wait for them. "I need a fence. Someone who can move diamonds."

"No problem."

"Someone who can move millions in diamonds."

Jake stopped leaning in his chair. "Problem."

"Can you solve it?"

Jake thought about it. "Yeah, but I need a few days."

"Fine. I'm going to need a backer, too. Someone who will front the whole job."

"I know some people."

"I'll need at least a hundred."

"Problem."

"Can you solve it?"

"It will take more than a few days."

"Fine."

"Wilson, that kind of money can come from only a few places, and the people who are willing to put that money out don't believe in collection agencies."

"Make it happen."

"Alright."

"And —"

"And?"

"I need someone who can sell me some diamonds."

CHAPTER ELEVEN

Miles was local, but I didn't catch him at home. I had to meet him at work. He smiled when he saw me and opened his hands in a wide arc as though he were Moses parting the sea instead of a crowded convention centre. "How many of these people do you think want to have sex with My Little Pony?"

"What?"

"You heard me."

"I heard what you said, but I don't follow." I looked at the posters and booths lined with children's toys and images of cartoon horses. Then I looked more closely at the people. There weren't any kids. There were hardly any women. "You can't mean."

Miles smiled. "Uh hunh. They're Bronies."

"Bronies?"

"Like ponies but with a *b*."

I shook my head. "And they all want to —"

"No, not all. That's why I want you to guess. Go ahead. You get within five percent, and I'll buy you dinner."

I looked around the room. The men were mostly white, mostly slightly overweight, and mostly pathetic. They gave off a last-picked-in-everything vibe. They were outsiders, each and every one of them, but wanting to sleep with a cartoon pony put them on the outside of even the outsiders. "Ten percent," I said.

"Not even close. It's thirty-eight."

One of my eyebrows raised. "You're making that up."

Miles laughed. "According to Bronyponies, the largest Brony fan site on this side of the Pacific, the last major convention of this size had an estimated 37.8 percent of attendees showing interest in having a relationship of a, let's call it, romantic nature with one of the ponies."

"They are that open about it?"

Miles shook his head. "It was an anonymous survey geared at making the next convention even better. I'm sure most never speak about wanting to turn the convention into a real petting zoo, but I'm guessing the remote possibility of getting a bit closer to *riding* one of the horses made most of the deviants a little bolder than usual."

"How do you know all this? Don't tell me you're one of the thirty-eight percent."

"Nope. I saw the survey on an internet news site and it got me thinking."

"About fucking a cartoon."

"No — about the people who want to fuck a cartoon. They even have a term for it. They call themselves cloppers."

I looked at the crowd. Really looked at the crowd. The demographic of mostly middle-aged white men meant that, statistically, they were likely to be employed. The fact that they were into My Little Pony meant they were probably single and likely loners. Loners with jobs meant disposable income. "What's the con?"

"Good to see you're up to speed. Riddle me this: what is the biggest impediment to wanting My Little Pony to be your girlfriend?"

"Two things — dimensions."

"Right," Miles said. "So what are you left with?"

"Porn," I said.

"Rule 34," Miles said.

"I don't follow."

"It's an internet thing. Rule 34 states: if it exists, there is porn about it. The ponies exist, therefore the porn is out there."

"But we are in here," I said. "And you . . ." I took another long look at the crowd, "you're selling them the porn."

"No, that would be sick. I'm selling them the prospect of porn, not the real thing. Otherwise, I'd have to go home at night and wash my eyes."

"Take me through it."

"The convention organizers are estimating two thousand attendees over the whole weekend."

"Seems steep for a cartoon convention."

"It does, but this convention — they call it the Brony Derby — only happens once every two years, and it's the only convention that gets some of the voice actors to show up."

"So roughly thirty-eight percent of the two thousand are into getting into the ponies."

"Right. Knowing that almost 750 marks will be in attendance, I started laying the groundwork online. I hit up chat rooms for a few months and put word on the binary street."

"You're selling porn," I said. "Porn with some kind of hook. Porn you can't get anywhere else."

"Bingo," Miles said. "You know what all of these people have in common?"

"Bed bugs," I said.

"Cash. Conventions are a cash business. These idiots are loaded with it and they are not shy about spending it. I set up a meeting spot in a nearby hotel bar and started taking orders. I asked for half up front."

"How much?"

"A hundred," Miles said.

"Low, but that's the point. They had already committed to the transaction when they showed up to meet with you; the low price makes them feel better about paying half up front for whatever you're selling."

"Genuine animation cells from the show that have been doctored by one of the show's original artists."

"How many bit on the offer?" I asked.

"Four hundred."

I let out a low whistle. He was on track to make forty grand. "It's a good scam, but it would have to be. You can't pull this off more than once. This community has to be so small that word would get out. No one will fall for this again."

"None of the Bronies, but the Sailor Moon crowd will."

I didn't know what a Sailor Moon was, but I didn't come out to talk fringe porn with the con man. "How about something a bit more adult?"

"You sure you don't want to get a megaphone and tell all the cloppers that I'm scamming them? That seems to be your thing these days."

"You still mad about me showing Johnny what was behind the curtain?"

"It was a dick move."

"It was unprofessional."

"Is that your way of saying you're sorry?"

"You were unprofessional. You don't con your crew. You save that for the civilians."

"He was a dick."

"He was still in on the job and that means he's off limits."

"Even if he's a dick."

"Yup."

"Even if he's a racist dick."

"Yup."

"I don't agree with that."

"Then walk away from the job. That's your choice. But you didn't choose to walk away. You chose to sign on. After that happens, every decision you make affects the crew. Conning the crew puts the job in danger. Worse, you put everyone in danger of getting killed or picked up. You don't get to make that choice for everyone."

"I still say he was a fucking dick."

"Grow up. I told you, the only quality a person in our line of work needs to have is reliability. They have to be able to do whatever they say they can do. If they can do that, you can put up with the rest until the job is done."

Miles took his eyes off the legions of dateless men. "You really believe that?"

"I'm here."

Miles laughed. "You calling me a dick?"

"I'm calling you a hell of a con man, and that's what the job needs."

Miles laughed. "Tell me about it."

CHAPTER TWELVE

Like Miles, Monica was local, but she wasn't based in New York. She worked a regular job at a go-kart track in Jersey. The track had a sign outside claiming that it was the biggest indoor track in America. The claim sounded impressive until you walked inside and saw that America's largest go-kart track was a tire-lined maze inside a warehouse. We found Monica in the garage, working on an overturned kart.

She looked up from the kart and appraised me through the lenses of her black-rimmed glasses. "And here I thought it was just a one-night stand." She looked at Miles. "A long boring one-night stand with far too much talking."

"And now you find out it was just a first date," Miles said.

"Lucky me."

"This place yours?" I asked.

Monica snorted. "If it was, I sure as hell wouldn't be working on one of these."

She put down her wrench and used a greasy rag to wipe her hands. I watched the rag move with practiced efficiency as she drove the grime up her fingers and off her hands. When she finished, she tossed the rag on top of the go-kart's tire. "C'mon, you can buy me lunch."

Lunch was a hot dog at the track concession stand. Monica ate with her blue coveralls unzipped and bunched around her waist. The cheap white T-shirt showed off her strong arms and the outline of a bra that looked like it might be something colourful and feminine. She started in on her food on her way back to the table and was halfway through her hot dog before anyone else had started theirs. She ate with a carelessness that wasn't really careless; her movements were quick, but precise. Every time I thought ketchup or mustard was about to stain her white undershirt, she darted her head forward and caught the oozing condiment with a small bite.

"Do you eat like this every day?" Miles asked. He had made it through half of his hot dog before he put it down and pushed it away.

"Only when someone else is buying. Otherwise, I skip lunch." She turned her small brown eyes on me. "So you got a job for me?"

"Maybe," I said.

"Maybe?"

"If you want it."

"Same thing we talked about?"

I shook my head. "You know why the job got called off?"

"Jake called me and told me it was off. Later, I saw David and Alvin's picture in the paper. I figured the job died with our inside man."

"It did," I said.

"And yet, here we are."

Miles gestured to Monica's lip. "You got a little ketchup there."

The driver licked her lips without any attempt at being provocative.

"That job is dead," I said. "Without an inside man, none of it will work. Any chance we had of getting inside is gone." I told them about what I had been doing with my time and what I had seen.

"So, he's as paranoid as David said he was," Monica said between bites of the rest of Miles's hot dog.

"No," Miles said.

"What?"

"Saul would be paranoid if he thought people were following him and there wasn't anyone doing it, but he was being followed. We've been on his tail for days. So, I don't think you can technically call him paranoid if he's right."

"Whatever," Monica said. "The point is the man is always looking over his shoulder."

"That's why we won't be able to get inside," I said.

"But you've been watching him, and you're here," Monica said. "So you have something in mind. How do we get at those diamonds if we can't get inside?"

"I have to admit," Miles said, "the question crossed my mind as well."

"We don't get in," I said.

"So we just wait for the stones to come to us?" Miles said.

"Close," I said. "We get Saul to bring them to us."

Miles made a face. "How do we get him to do that?"

"Simple," I said. "We tell him what happened to David."

CHAPTER THIRTEEN

"You really think that will work?" Monica said.

We were back in her shop and she was back in her coveralls, elbow deep in a carburetor.

"Yes," I said.

Miles spun the handle on a table vice. "What do we have to lose if we try?"

Monica shrugged as she worked a wrench against a stubborn nut. "Nothing really. Just all the money that was fronted for this thing to work. This thing goes south — and let's face it, it could go south easy — we're out a hundred K."

"Even if we sold off what we bought, we'd be selling it at a loss, and there's also the vig to consider," Miles said.

"There's always risk," I said.

"That's only if things go bad. If everything goes right, we're up a couple million."

"If it goes right," Monica said. "And that is a very big if."

"It will," Miles said. "Tell her, Wilson."

"Risk versus reward," I said. "The bigger the risk, the

bigger the reward. You want a guaranteed return, go buy a savings bond."

"Well, if that doesn't convince her, I don't know what will," Miles said.

"No," she said. "He's right. Fine, I'm in."

"Almost," I said.

Monica's eyes widened; it might have been surprise, but it could have just as easily been anger. "Almost?"

"I want to see you behind the wheel," I said.

The driver smiled wide. "No problem. I get off at —"

"Now," I said.

"Now? I got work to do. I can't go driving around town."

"Not around town," I said. "Around the track."

Monica laughed. "You want to watch me drive the course?"

"No," I said. "I want to watch you race the course."

"Against who?"

I looked at Miles. "Against him."

CHAPTER FOURTEEN

At two o'clock on a Thursday, it wasn't hard to find an open slot in the track schedule. The kid working at the gate wore a shirt decorated like a checkered flag with the words *Pit Crew* stencilled on the back. The shirt was two sizes too big, and the kid didn't bother trying to hide it. The uniform hung like a dress over his skin-tight jeans. The kid was leaning against the gate that allowed access to the track and sliding his thumbs all over the surface of a cell phone. Monica made a noise and the kid looked up from his phone. He moved over and said a quiet, "'Sup," before getting back to his phone.

Miles followed Monica, but he pulled up short when he saw the helmets. He balked at the idea of wearing a helmet, but Monica ignored him and stepped up to the rack behind the counter and strapped one on. She didn't bother examining the karts to find the fastest machine; she got behind the wheel of the first kart in line and revved the engine. I heard the motor whine under the pressure of her foot and watched as she interpreted the language of the small combustible engine. Whatever she heard made her grin; the compact smile echoed in the lines that formed in the corners of her eyes.

Miles flashed a smile of his own as he got behind the wheel of his kart. He revved the engine until the sound hurt my ears and then pulled alongside Monica. The driver gave the con man a glance and then turned her eyes back to the red light. Miles said something over the noise of the engines, but Monica didn't respond. She cared only about the green.

A group of college students passed me. The kid on the phone took his eyes off the screen long enough to get the trio helmets and point them towards the karts.

Monica noticed the new drivers getting behind the wheels of the go-karts and looked over at the kid on his phone. She had to yell his name a couple of times before he pulled his eyes away from the texts that had captured his attention. Monica yelled, "Give us a minute, Frankie."

The pit crew member nodded and held up an open palm to the college students.

One of the kids said, "What the fuck?"

Monica looked over her shoulder and spoke just as loud. "Private race. It'll be over in a minute."

The college kids wanted to gripe more about it, but Monica fed her kart some gas and the little engine showed that it still could.

The pit crew member put his phone in his back pocket and fiddled with a control panel. Lights on the track went red, and yellow followed seconds later. The wait for green lasted ten long seconds before the light changed. Miles stomped on the gas and his tires spun on the track until the warm rubber found purchase. His car jolted forward and he set off down the track in second place. Monica, already twenty meters ahead of the con man, tore into the first turn without any hint of slowing down. She glided through the turn, utilizing both lanes to navigate the elbow bend in the track. Her body leaned into and out of the turn, and the kart missed the tires lining the side of the track by inches. Miles hit the same turn seconds after. A few seconds after that, he collided with the tires. The kart skidded sideways into the rubber, and the impact briefly sent the cart onto two wheels.

I looked at the college kids and said, "You can go now." The trio needed no further encouragement. Engines whined in *Texas Chainsaw Massacre* enthusiasm. The pit crew member looked up from his phone and saw that the college kids were ready to give chase. I nodded towards the lights and then stared at the kid until he initiated the sequence. On the green, three karts exploded off the line. The three go-karts pounded into the tires of the first turn like a Mike Tyson body blow. I could see the college kids laugh and hoot as they muscled themselves out of the turn and onto the straightaway.

Farther up the track, Monica was carving through the turns with the precision of a surgeon with OCD. Her body swayed with the motion of the kart as she forced it to move with an elegance that should have been foreign to such a utilitarian machine. Behind her, Miles attempted to use power to overcome his lack of finesse. On the final straight-away, Monica came out of the turn and let the engine loose.

She was easing off the throttle when she noticed my hand pointing down the track. The smile disappeared and the throttle came back in an angry hornet's drone. I watched Monica pass me and then I looked back at the track. I ignored Miles's progress and instead focused on the college kids. They were just passing the halfway mark and were still intent on treating the go-karts like bumper cars.

Monica had covered more than a quarter of the track when Miles pulled to a stop in front of me and pulled off his helmet. "Did I win?"

I shook my head and kept my eyes on the track as Monica closed in on the college kids. She eased off the gas as she came out of a sharp turn and her momentum carried her within feet of the two slowest drivers. One of the pair used the straight stretch of track to veer left and then hard to the right. He drove the side of his kart into his friend and the two laughed as they rebounded off one another and flirted with the tires lining the track. Monica left the wake of the pair ahead of her and accelerated through the temporary hole they had left in the middle of the lane. The third driver heard the shouts of his friends that they had been lapped and flashed a look over his shoulder. He saw Monica and made a split-second decision that he wasn't going to get lapped, too. The lead kart drifted into the centre of the lane and increased its speed. Monica edged closer on the right side, but the kid saw her coming and put his bumper in front of her. Monica eased off the gas as they came into the final turn; her opponent showed no sign of taking his foot off of the accelerator. The college kid's tires screeched as he barely managed to hold the kart on the track. He scraped the tires but lost little of his speed. Monica kept her kart hugging the opposite side of the track. The positioning put Monica in line with the rear tires of the other kart. I waited for the engines to respond to both pedals kissing the floor as the two drivers raced to the finish line, but I got a different sound from down the track. The kid went for the finish line; Monica hit the gas and angled left into the thin bumper inches away. The impact just behind the rear tire of the kid's car combined with his overcompensation coming out of the last turn forced the winning kart into a spin. Monica maneuvered by the other car as it came dangerously close to tipping and crossed the finish line in first place. If she cared about the fate of the other driver, I couldn't tell.

She decelerated without squealing the tires and got out. I couldn't see it under the helmet, but I knew that there was a smile there.

"You're in."

CHAPTER FIFTEEN

I spent the next morning watching the outside of the jewellery store. At eleven, I drove out of the city to Greenburgh. I followed the directions Jake had given me and pulled into the lot of T&C Builder's Supply at one in the afternoon. There were three trucks parked close to the lot's entrance; two of them sported company names on their doors. I pulled in next to a black Ford belonging to a contractor and checked the lot. The squat square building ahead of me fronted a huge fenced-in yard that contained a dozen neatly lined yellow flatbed trucks sporting the letters *T* and *C* on the side. The rest of the yard contained stacks of bricks arranged in neat uniform columns.

I walked inside and asked for Ron. A middle-aged woman listening to light hits of the late eighties pointed to the back door with the invoice she was holding in her right hand. I wandered the aisles of stacked bricks and concrete forms, following the sound of a forklift somewhere near the back of the yard. I found Ron off-loading a shipment of bricks. He moved the forklift quickly from truck to pallet, pausing only to spit out of the opening to his right. He caught my eye and finished moving the bricks he had in the air. He wheeled the forklift around so that he could look at me from the opening to his left, killed the engine, and spoke to me from the driver's seat.

"Something you need?"

"You Ron?"

The guy behind the wheel was in his fifties with the red-veined face of a drinker. The wad of tobacco in his cheek strained the flesh of his face, forming the only taught spot his body possessed; the rest of him was flabby. "I'm Ron. What can I help you with?"

"I'm looking for iron," I said, using the words Jake had told me to say. He also told me what would come next.

"We don't sell iron here. All we have is brick and stone."

He moved to start the forklift. I could tell he was moving slow enough to offer me time to respond.

"How about lead?"

Ron nodded and spat before getting out of the forklift. "Follow me."

We walked through the stacks until the columns became piles. In the far corner of the lot, surrounded by broken company vehicles and far away from the legitimate side of the business, was a rusted shipping container. Ron opened the door and stepped inside. He had vanished in the darkness only to reappear in the light of an old camping lantern. I stepped to the door frame and saw the gun in Ron's hand.

"Shirt up."

I didn't fight it. I was told there would be a search and that I needed to let it happen if I wanted to do business. I pulled up my shirt and turned in a circle to show Ron that I wasn't wired.

"Who sent you here?"

"A fun guy."

The answer was the right one. He put the gun into the pocket of his jacket. "What do you need?"

"Three guns. Two need to be police issue. The third can be anything reliable."

Ron rubbed at the stubble on his chin. "Police means 9 mm. You have a choice of Sig, Glock, or Smith & Wesson. I can get you the Glock or the Sig right away. S&Ws can be done, but it will take a little time."

"Can you do two of both?"

"I only have one Sig."

"I'll take all three."

"You want to test them?"

I nodded.

"Alright. Wait here."

Ron walked out of the container, and a minute later I heard the forklift start up. The sound of the moving machine made me curious enough to step outside. I followed the sound two rows over and found Ron standing next to a column of bricks. The forklift was still running and its tongs were busy keeping a couple thousand pounds of bricks from falling on Ron's head. From a space inside the stack of bricks, Ron pulled out a case. He walked the case back to the forklift and lowered the bricks back down to the column. I walked back to the container before Ron noticed me and waited for him to repeat his actions on another pallet of bricks elsewhere in the yard. Five minutes later, Ron walked back to the shipping container carrying two cases.

Inside the cases were two Glocks, a Sig, and two revolvers.

"The revolvers are S&Ws, but they won't pass for police issue."

I looked over the revolvers. "The four inch is a .38. The smaller —"

"That's a .22," Ron said.

"Where can I test them?"

"You can shoot them right here." He walked to the other side of the container and turned on another camping light; the burst of illumination revealed rows of sandbags against the far wall of the container. He pulled two sets of earmuffs from an empty milk crate and walked a pair back to me.

"These will take care of the noise for you and me, and this is for everyone else." He stepped outside the container, and a few seconds later a gas generator started. Ron came back in and closed the door behind him. "No one is going to hear anything over that. You want the Glock first?"

I nodded and Ron put on his earmuffs before handing me the weapon and a box of 9 mm bullets. I took my time loading both weapons. They were well maintained and without a lot of wear and tear. "They clean?"

"They didn't come that way, but the serial numbers are gone and I changed the barrels on both of them."

I worked the slide and lifted the gun to shoulder height. The earmuffs didn't work as well as I had hoped they would.

"Nice, right?"

I ignored Ron and the ringing in my ears and picked up the second Glock. The trigger pulled easier on the second gun, but it did the job just as well.

I picked up the .38 and loaded a bullet into the cylinder. I closed the gun with my palm and aimed down the length of the container. The .38 had more of a kick than the Glock, but it shot straight.

"Twenty-five for the two Glocks and the .38."

Ron rubbed at his chin and it moved three inches. "Three."

"Twenty-eight with the ammunition and something to carry them in."

Ron thought about it for a few seconds before he said, "Deal."

CHAPTER SIXTEEN

I met Miles and Monica back at the motel room. One of the great things about New York is the seemingly endless number of cash motels. It doesn't matter where you are, you're never far from a place that will accept cash for a bed. I had been selective about the room and had opted for a place that offered monthly rates and had rooms with kitchens and living rooms that would seem cramped in Barbie's dream house. The space was tight for one, but it somehow managed to accommodate several large families in the complex.

I had the guns on the kitchen table next to the IDs Miles had picked up. The work was good.

"Your guy knows his stuff."

"For what we're paying him, he should. They'll hold up to an inspection by anyone, even a cop, but if they check the information it'll come up bunko."

"I know," I said. "It won't come to that."

Miles nodded at Monica. "You tell him?"

"About the car? Yeah, he knows I'm going to pick up the

Crown Vic tonight."

"You really think she should bring it back here?" Miles asked.

I got up and pulled a magnetic sign from a drawer. I had picked it up after I met with Ron. I handed the flimsy magnet to Miles and sat back down.

"What the hell is Donovan Security?"

"An excuse for a car that looks like a police car. In the lot, people will just take it for a private security car. When we want people to think differently, we'll take it off."

Miles looked around the room. "So I guess we're working tomorrow."

"Morning and night. We leave here at four."

"Four?"

"I want him to see us get out of the car. For that to happen, we need to be early enough to get a parking space on his route."

Miles didn't argue. He understood that if Saul was going to buy our story, his brain would need to be our accomplice. We had to feed his mind everything it needed to create its own idea. If his brain took in badges, guns, and a police car on its own, it would have less trouble ingesting our story.

"Is there a hydrant on the street? Or some kind of no parking sign?" Miles asked.

"There's a hydrant."

"We should park in front of that. Cops don't follow traffic laws. It's one of the things people hate most about them."

"It's true," Monica said. "You ever see one of them stop before they pull right on a red?"

I grinned. Miles was right.

"We'll get a spot to be safe, but we should pull in front of the hydrant when Saul shows. We can brace him right there," Miles said.

I shook my head. "We get him into the car and drive him around while we talk to him."

It was Miles's turn to smile. "I like it."

CHAPTER SEVENTEEN

The morning was a bust. Firing that last guard had made the other two as punctual as the tall hats outside Buckingham Palace. The two guards were on the stairs and in view of the fire hydrant a minute before Saul had even parked his car. The night was more accommodating.

Through binoculars, I watched the jewellery store clear out. Just like clockwork, the receptionist and jewellers cleared out first, followed by Saul and the security guards ten minutes later. The guards followed the same route they used every other time I had watched them. There were curt nods all around, and then Saul and his security parted ways. It was just after eight when the jeweller started down the street towards us. There was a slight breeze, and the wind opened the old man's coat. I leaned in and tried to train the binoculars on the jeweller, but there were too many people between us for me to get a look at what the old man was carrying on his hip.

"You worried he'll shoot us?"

"Us?"

"Fine," Miles said. "Are you at all worried that he'll shoot me?"

"A little."

"Wait. What?"

I pulled out of the parking spot and drove up the street. I got ahead of Saul, but that didn't matter — I knew where he was going.

I pulled up in front of a fire hydrant and watched the rear-view; Miles used the side mirror. We saw the jeweller emerge from behind a couple holding hands who stopped to look at a window display. We let Saul get a little closer, and then we opened the doors.

"Badges," I said.

I held up my badge and waited a second for Miles to catch up.

"Mr. Mendelson, my name is Detective Lock and this is Detective Croft. We'd like you to come with us."

Saul paused and looked at me while the rest of the street ran at regular speed.

I put the badge in an inner pocket as I rounded the rear bumper so that Saul could get a look at the gun in the shoulder holster.

"Sir, you *need* to come with us."

Saul picked up on the emphasis I put on the word need and came out of his trance.

"Am I under arrest?"

Miles tucked his badge into his coat and gave Saul a view of the identical Glock that he was carrying in a matching shoulder holster. "Nothing like that, sir." He looked up and down the street and then rechecked the sidewalk. "We would just rather have this conversation in private."

"What kind of conversation?"

"We have reason to believe that someone is planning to rob your jewellery store, and we would like you to help us stop it."

Everything that I had learned about Saul came second-hand from his protegé. So far it seemed a lot of what David had told me about his boss and his place of employment was true. The store functioned the way David said it did and Saul kept to the schedule David told us about in his basement. Watching the jeweller's comings and goings told me that David was right about something else — the old man was paranoid. Paranoia was a second shadow that followed Saul wherever he went. Mentioning a threat to the store uprooted the jeweller's feet and brought him to us. He gave our badges a once-over and then looked over his shoulder for some unseen threat. The momentary glance gave me a chance to look at the gun Saul was carrying. The hip holster was an ornate custom leather job that left only the golden butt of the small custom gun visible.

"You want *me* to help *you*? I don't understand."

"It would be better if we talked about this in the car, sir."

Saul took a step towards the car but apprehension pulled him back. "Let me see your identification again."

Miles looked at me, and I shrugged. I pulled my badge out of my pocket and opened it for Saul. Miles followed suit, and we spent a long minute waiting for Saul to review our credentials. Saul nodded and we put away our badges. The old man waited until my hand was out of my coat before he said, "What's your badge number?"

I recited the number on my way back to the car. Without waiting to be asked, Miles did the same on his way to the rear door. He opened it and motioned for Saul to get inside.

"Unless you want to ask me when my birthday is first."

CHAPTER EIGHTEEN

"**W**hat is going on?"

I turned onto 48th and spoke over my shoulder without taking my eyes off the road. "We have reason to believe that there is a plan to rob your store. We think it's already in motion."

"What?"

Miles turned and fit his head through the space between the seats, "We have reason to believe —"

"I heard you. I was just shocked."

The car filled with silence for thirty seconds; I didn't try to let it out. The quiet gave Saul's mind all the room it needed to start running.

"Who is going to rob the store?"

Miles sighed. "We don't know."

"When are they going to do it?"

"We don't know that, either," Miles said.

"You pull me off the street, tell me my business is going to be robbed, and now I find out you don't know who or when. This is insane."

I lifted my eyes from the road and looked at Saul in the rear-view mirror. "Sir," I said.

"No, this is insane. Take me back."

"Sir."

"I said take me back. You can't tell me a single thing about this so-called robbery."

"We didn't say that," I said.

"What?"

"We didn't say we couldn't tell you a single thing. We just don't know those details," I said.

"Well, what do you know?"

"For one thing," Miles said. "We know it's an inside job."

CHAPTER NINETEEN

"**W**hat the hell are you talking about? You're saying one of my employees is trying to steal from me?" Saul laughed. "I don't believe it."

"I know this must be a shock, Mr. Mendelson, but it's the truth," I said.

"Tell me how this can be the truth. Tell me how you can be so sure that one of *my* employees is planning on robbing my store."

"We were recently contacted by an employee of your store. Now, when I say we, I don't mean us. A call was logged and the details were taken down by one of the people working our phones. Now, you have to understand —" I took my eyes off the road long enough to look at Saul, "we get calls like this all the time. All the time. The information gets logged and the information gets passed on. Not to us. The information gets passed on to our supervisors and they hand it out to us if they think it is pertinent."

"Who called you? It sure as hell wasn't me."

I ignored the question. "A second call was placed about a potential robbery, and when the tip was logged, the computer linked it to the first call we received a few weeks before. The information was forwarded up the chain again. Let me say again, we get calls like this all the time. We have a stack of them on our desk as we speak."

"Yeah, yeah, yeah. I get it. You're very busy. Just cut to the chase. Which one of my people called you?"

I turned my head and looked at Saul again before I spoke. "The call came from David Phillips."

Saul sat back in his seat and let his neck go slack. "David," he said slowly, as though the noun had a physical weight.

"Yes," I said. "It was Mr. Phillips who left us the messages."

"He never told me about any of this."

"His messages indicated that the persons involved were dangerous. We've come to believe that he didn't want to endanger you by getting you involved."

"It's my business," Saul said.

"He was protecting you," I said.

"He was a sweet boy. He was always looking out for me. Calling you sounds just like him. But why are you so interested now. You didn't believe him when he first called you, but now, all of a sudden, you tell me that he was right. What changed?"

"We got some new evidence," I said. "The evidence backed up what David had told us."

"What evidence is this?"

"It came out of the accident reconstruction team."

"Accident reconstruction? You mean David's accident? What does a car accident have to do with this?"

I counted three Mississippis in my head before I answered. "We don't believe it was an accident that killed David. We believe he was murdered."

CHAPTER TWENTY

"**W**hat?"

"The car was run off the road. The death has been ruled a homicide. The detectives found out about the messages left by David, and they think that his knowledge of a plot to rob your store was the motive for the murder."

"The messages you did nothing about."

"Sir, you have to understand, we get so many —"

"Calls," Saul finished. "I understand just fine. David is dead because your answering machine was full."

I understood just fine, too. Saul had decided to shoot the messenger.

I softened my voice and tried again. "Mr. Mendelson —"

Saul cut me off. "I loved that boy like a son — like a son. To you, he was just some guy on the phone you could ignore, but to me —"

"We know how much David meant to you and how much he did for your business."

"Oh, you know do you?" Saul made a derisive snort. "You don't know anything."

I looked over at Miles and he subtly lifted his palm. He wanted me to let him cut in. I looked over at Saul who was consciously ignoring me and nodded.

"Mr. Mendelson," Miles said, "we have no excuse for what happened. None. A good man is dead and we know that we played a part in that. It was a small part, but we hold ourselves responsible. We can't change what happened — that's beyond our power. But we can do something for David; we can find the people who did this and we can bring them to justice. That justice belongs to David, and we intend to give it to him. But we can't do it without you. Please help us do what we should have done from the start. Help us stop this robbery. Help us catch the people responsible for what happened to David."

This was it. We had put every domino in place and we needed Saul to knock over the first one. Minutes went by in long stretches of silence broken by the sniffles of a man trying his best to hold it together. The quiet ended with a wet clearing of the throat and the words, "Let's get the sons of bitches."

CHAPTER TWENTY-ONE

"I still don't understand how you don't know who is trying to rob me. David called you. He didn't give you a name?"

We had stopped at a Dunkin' Donuts in Hell's Kitchen and picked up coffees and a plain doughnut for Saul. The free food did nothing to soften Saul. "David had suspicions," I said. "He knew in his gut that something was going on, but he wasn't one hundred percent sure. That happens more than you think. People think someone they know is up to something, but they're hesitant to say anything out of the fear that they're wrong."

"He gave you nothing?"

I was driving towards the Hudson and nursing the bitter coffee. I put the cup down and looked at Saul in the rear-view. Even though I had been talking to him, he was looking at Miles whenever he said anything. It was clear that he was taking out whatever anger he had about David's death on me. He blamed me and I was starting to wonder if he always would. Miles read Saul's anger and took over the conversation as smoothly as a lane change on the highway.

"He gave us his name, not the store's name, or yours, just his name. He told us his line of work and that he suspected some of his co-workers were planning to rob the store. He brought up how important it was that this matter stayed confidential. That was really important to him."

"But why wouldn't he tell me?"

"He was probably looking out for your health."

"My health?" Saul said. "What's wrong with my health?"

I didn't turn my head from the bumper in front of me, but from the corner of my eye I caught the look Miles shot me. He knew he had fucked up, but there were no apologies in this line of work and no way to put a genie back in the bottle. I kept my eyes on the car in front of me and took my foot off the gas when the brake lights shone red.

"I'm sorry," Miles said. "I know it's a sensitive subject."

"What?" Saul demanded. "What is a sensitive subject?"

Miles didn't answer. Instead he took a sip of his coffee and elbowed my arm. "This doesn't taste like two sugars. Are you sure you don't have mine?"

Saul raised his voice, "What is a sensitive subject?"

Miles put his coffee in the cup holder and took a few seconds to make sure Saul knew he was uncomfortable with the subject. He faced Saul and softened his voice. "David mentioned that you have been forgetting things lately."

"Forgetting things?"

"Yes, sir. Those were his words. At least, that was how it was taken down in the notes. He used the phrase *taking advantage of him* a couple of times."

"It's not something we should have brought up," I said.

"He was just being honest," Saul snapped. "I appreciate honesty. I respect it."

"I should have been more considerate," Miles said.

"No, you were doing your job," Saul said. "I was angry at you before for not doing it; it would be crazy for me to be upset that you are doing it now."

Miles turned around in his seat. "How are things with you?"

Saul made some noise opening the paper bag holding his doughnut. He took a bite and chewed thoughtfully. "I am seventy-four years old. I am an old man. That's not so bad. Many people don't get to be old. What's bad is the knowing. I know I'm old. I also know that there are days when I am not as sharp as I once was. It's like you said, I forget things — but those days come and go and then I'm back to being myself."

"Thank you for being so honest," Miles said. "Could I ask you another question?"

"You want to know if I get up to pee during the night? Well, I already told you I'm old, so you can figure that out for yourself."

Miles laughed. "This one isn't personal. I wanted to know if anything has struck you as odd lately. Y'know, people following you or maybe just a feeling that you're being watched."

Saul drank some more coffee and thought about it. Finally, he said, "No, nothing, but I've been too busy lately to notice anything. With David's funeral and running the store, I haven't been able to find the time to sit down."

"Must be tough," Miles said.

"David was my right hand. I had forgotten how much work it took to run a business like this. To be honest, I've been racked with guilt. I never realized how much David really did for me. I should have retired years ago. And now, without David, I can't."

David had organized the robbery because he thought his time would never come, and it turned out that the only person standing in his way had been him.

"We know that David suspected someone on the inside and that he wanted to protect you," I said. "That means you're the only person that we can trust."

Saul reached over the seat and put his hand on Miles's shoulder. "What do you need me to do?"

"Right now, we just need you to be our eyes and ears. We're working the case hard, sir. We'll have a lead soon."

"You said that David never gave you any real information."

"You only have a handful of employees," I said. "We are looking into all of them. If there is something there, we'll find it."

"Like what?"

"It could be anything from a record to being a known associate of a criminal."

"And if you find them, you can arrest them."

"Not quite," I said.

Saul shook his head dismissively at me. "Then what?"

"Having a suspicion isn't enough," Miles said. "We need more. That's where you come in."

"At more?"

"When the time is right, we want you to help us get the kind of evidence no one could refute."

"And how do I help you get that?" Saul asked.

"By helping us catch them in the act," Miles said.

CHAPTER TWENTY-TWO

We dropped Saul off at his car and told him we would be in touch. We also told him to call us if he noticed anything that might help with our investigation. Saul held up the phony business card we had given him and said that he would.

When he closed the door, Miles spoke under his breath, "What do you think?"

I thought about it. "He was more lucid than I expected. A little meaner, too."

"Maybe to you," Miles said. "But I know what you mean. David gave us the impression that the old guy was driving the business into the ground with both hands, but the man we met tonight wasn't some fuddy-duddy. He was shrewd. You see the way he checked our badge numbers? That was clever. I thought maybe he'd make us repeat them while he looked at the numbers, but that old coot memorized both badge numbers. That's hard to do if you've lost your marbles."

"He might not have memorized them," I said. "He might have just wanted us to think he did, or that he still could.

He could have just watched for our reactions. A hesitation could have been as good as a fail."

Miles nodded his head. "Maybe, but I got the impression that he had those numbers down cold."

"Me too," I said.

"So that leaves us with a question."

"Two," I said.

"Two?"

"Did Saul have a lucid hour with us, or was David not telling us the whole story?"

CHAPTER TWENTY-THREE

The next day, we let Saul see us parked on the street as he walked to work. Saul played it cool and didn't give us a second glance. Of course, there was a possibility that he didn't remember us.

The next night, Monica tailed him home. She followed him and worked hard to be obvious about it. We had no idea if Saul ever looked in his rear-view, but we wanted to be there if it happened. It turned out, Saul was nothing like other people his age. He kept his eyes on his mirrors and his hands at ten and two.

"I did what you said," Monica told us when she got back to the motel room. "I came up on him a block from his parking garage and put my bumper up his ass."

"Did he notice you?" Miles asked.

"By the third turn he was on to me."

"What'd he do?"

"Sped up and started driving more aggressively. He cruised through a red light and came this close to getting T-boned." Monica smiled as she mimicked the distance with her thumb and index finger. "For a second, it felt like déjà vu — derailed by another car wreck — but the old guy squeaked through."

"How did you play it?" I asked.

Monica took a swig of her beer, then said, "I stopped at the light."

"Good," I said. Saul was panicked, and that was where we needed him to be. Seeing Monica following him again the next night would increase the pressure.

"Follow him again tomorrow, but be a bit subtler about it."

"I thought you wanted it to be obvious."

"At first, but now he'll be looking for you. He knows that you know he made you. The natural response would be to avoid letting that happen again, but we need it to happen again."

"So you want me to get caught looking like I'm trying not to get caught."

"Yes."

"I can do that." Monica got off her chair and put what was left of her beer in the sink. She searched four cupboards and found each one bare. "Don't you have anything to eat?"

"I don't think he eats," Miles said. "If he does, it would have to be something you can eat while scowling. Maybe spaghetti."

Monica shoved her hands into her jeans' pockets. The faded denim was tight and spotted with dirt and grease stains around the knees. She pulled an equally worn denim jacket off a chair and pulled it on. "Well, I'm going for food."

"Can I join you?" Miles asked.

"Better — you can buy me dinner."

"Like a date."

"Like a lease on the seat beside me."

Miles shrugged. "It's more room than my apartment." He grabbed his coat and went for the door. He looked at me before he opened it and said, "Tomorrow?"

"I got the morning shift but be ready for closing time."

"Sounds like a plan."

CHAPTER TWENTY-FOUR

The next day, we put in appearances on the street for Saul and then drove to Tommy's Super Fantastic Funporium. It had rained a couple of hours before and the puddles were bouncing the discarded light up into our faces.

Miles smirked as we walked toward the bar. "They say the secret of good taste is knowing when to stop."

"He says all the flash is his cover."

"Maybe," Miles said. "Or maybe Jake just couldn't take the idea of people not knowing how super-fantastic he is."

We stepped out of the artificial light and into a dim womb created by the few feet in between the two sets of doors separating the bar and the street. I put my hand on the door and readied my senses for an assault from all of the fun waiting to strike.

"How much do you think he'll want?"

It was a fair question. Of all the job's weak points, this was the most tender. The job hinged on a switch. I needed to trade Saul for what he had in his safe, and a trade for millions in diamonds wouldn't come cheap. I had thought about using replicas, but we needed something of value to put up if we wanted Saul to continue to think we were legit. "Depends."

"On what?"

"On how many people it will take to get us what we want. The more people involved, the more we'll have to pay."

"We'll just have to hope that Jake really is super-fantastic."

We found Jake in his office, reading the newspaper while slurping down Chinese noodles slathered in a dark sauce. I guessed the food was off the bar menu. There was no aged masseuse-in-training rubbing his back this time. If the waitress had been there, she would have likely scolded Jake for hunching his shoulders so much.

Jake glanced at me and spoke with his mouth full. "You're early."

"He's always early," Miles said. "It's his thing."

Jake tilted his head to get a look over my shoulder at Miles. He dropped the newspaper and pointed a finger at Miles. "That is your only fuckin' warning, mouth. Another word out of you and I'll have one of the bouncers throw you out on the sidewalk — headfirst like a lawn dart."

Before Miles could open his mouth, Jake said, "Don't think okays don't count."

Miles closed his mouth and mimed locking it with an invisible key.

"Don't push it, mouth."

Jake was a criminal Rolodex who connected like-minded people with one another. More than helping people find others who were in the same line of work, Jake provided reliability. Jake guaranteed people who could do what they said they could do. But sometimes, making connections wasn't enough. Occasionally, Jake provided a neutral ground for people to introduce themselves and feel each other out. The Funporium was used as a place to meet because the light, noise, and sheer improbability of the location made it as safe from the eyes and ears of the law as the surface of the moon. Miles had taken advantage of Jake's willingness to let people use the Funporium as a means of networking and the free drinks he provided while they did it. Miles had set up jobs just to drink for free at the bar. He also let pretty girls drink for free, too. To be fair, Miles was using the bar to plan a robbery; he was just planning to rob the bar of all the liquor he could ingest.

"Who are we here to meet?" I asked.

Jake gave Miles a bit more of his best hard stare before looking back at me. Jake was a go-between, but the scar tissue around his eyes and his crooked nose let anyone who could read the signs know he hadn't always been a middle-man. "I told you when you called me back. I got someone lined up. You need stones and a fence. Well, this guy could potentially help you with both of your problems. Whatever name he wants to give you is his business."

"You going to be that secretive about his price?"

"That's what I wanted to talk to you about. The thing is —"

"How much?" I asked.

"Hear me out will ya?"

"How much?"

"Nothing, alright? At least not money anyway."

"What does he want?"

Before Jake could answer, Miles said, "He wants us to do a job. Whenever anyone is coy about price, it's because they want to bargain. What else do we have to bargain with?"

"What did I tell you about talking in my place?"

I held up my hand. "What does he owe you?"

Jake looked at Miles. "His tab is four grand."

I looked at Miles; he shrugged. "There was a bachelorette party. How was I supposed to know softball players could drink more than sailors?"

"The four comes out of our end."

Jake looked at Miles and a smile replaced the scowl. "Well, I guess that means he can talk whenever he wants."

"Is he right? Are we paying in cash or in work?"

Jake leaned back in his chair. His button-down shirt lifted and revealed white skin decorated with hair and stretch marks. "He has a job he needs done, alright? He'll tell you more when he shows up in an hour."

"If I can talk again," Miles said, "can I drink, too?"

"Get out."

CHAPTER TWENTY-FIVE

Jake had reserved a table for us in the far corner of the lower level of the bar. Miles had wanted to play some games, but I wasn't interested, so he drank instead. Starting the tab back at zero was clearly a challenge to the con man, and he was teaming up with vodka to meet it. As I watched Miles put down vodka after vodka, I wondered what other bad habits Miles was working to keep in check.

"The bill you ran up was hefty."

Miles shrugged. The handsome con man managed to make the gesture graceful. "What can I say, I hate drinking alone."

I felt eyes on me and immediately knew that the women around us were looking at Miles. "How much of that four G's was you and how much was hating to drink alone?"

Miles put down his glass on the table. "What are you getting at?"

I pointed at the glass. "How much are you drinking these days?"

"You worried about me?"

"When you're on the job I am."

"That's touching. It's just the kind of sentiment I'd expect from a man who shot an unarmed man in the chest."

I didn't flinch at the words. The loud din of the bar made everything Miles said unrecognizable to anyone who wasn't sitting on the other side of the table.

"But vodka isn't what you're really asking about, is it?"

"Nope," I said.

"Come right out and say it then, Wilson."

"Is it just the booze?"

"If you mean coke, I haven't used since Buffalo. Alright?"

I first connected with Miles on a job out of Buffalo. We were part of a crew out to steal a nineteenth century violin. Miles had kept his drug addiction quiet and it had almost cost him his life. His wits had kept him alive, and when it all hit the fan he saved my life, and the job. I jutted my chin towards the empty glass. "The booze?"

"What about it?"

"You haven't used since Buffalo, but you're drinking more."

"Am I? You sure about that because you know me so well?"

I said nothing.

Miles sighed. "The drinking is not a big deal. I can stop whenever I want to. Look —"

Miles picked up his glass off the table and held it out to me; I didn't take it.

"Take it."

When I didn't reach for it, he turned the glass and slammed it down on the table. A waiter within earshot turned his head towards us. "Hey, you can't slam your glass down on the table like that in here — oh, hey, Miles."

Miles smiled at the waiter. "Hey, Devon."

Devon looked like an action figure that had just been removed from the package. "You know that the boss said your tab is done, right?"

"I heard," Miles said. "But I talked to him, and we're cool now."

The waiter smiled wide. "Oh, yeah?"

"Check if you don't believe me."

The waiter put two elbows on the table and leaned into the space between us. "I have to, Miles. You know how it is. But if you're on the level," Devon gestured with a tilt of his head to another table, "there are some girls over there who are a lot of fun. Maybe you should think about sending them something to, y'know, get the ball rolling?"

Miles looked at me. The look wasn't for permission; it was the kind of look that said, *told you so*. When he felt he had made his point, he looked at the waiter and said, "Not tonight, Devon. My friend and I are meeting an old buddy."

The waiter's smile stayed on his face, but the mischievous fire lighting it went out. "Maybe tomorrow."

The disappointed waiter walked away, and Miles loaded a clever remark into the chamber. I lifted my palm and stopped him before he unloaded it on me. Whatever he wanted to say would have to wait because I saw a man coming down the stairs. He was in his late-fifties and balding. The hair loss created a shiny runway down the centre of his head. But it wasn't the man's age or receding hairline that drew looks from the much younger crowd, it was his height — his lack of height, really — that got him all of the attention.

I watched the man's stunted legs nimbly get him from the bottom of the stairs to our corner table. He stopped in front of us and looked from me to Miles and then back to me.

"Which one of you is Moriarty?"

Miles snorted.

"You?"

Miles shook his head.

"That makes you Ripley."

"I guess it does," Miles said.

The short man held out a fat hand and Miles took it. "Donny."

After he shook my hand, Donny looked the room over and said, "When Jake told me the meeting was here, I thought he was kidding. You mind if I sit down?"

"We're just getting up."

"You kidding me? I just got here. Wait, did I do something wrong?"

"This isn't the place for a meeting," I said.

Donny looked at the two of us. "Jake never said anything about me going anywhere with you guys."

"Relax," I said. "We're just going over there."

Donny followed my nod and looked over his shoulder. "You serious?"

Miles nodded. "If you're still worried, you can ask the waitress to keep an eye on you while we cross the room."

CHAPTER TWENTY-SIX

"I haven't played this since I was ten," Donny said. "I can't even remember if I'm holding these things right."

The dartboard was a forgotten relic in the corner of the Funporium. Not a single person had glanced at it while Miles and I had been in the bar. Everyone was more interested in carnival games with flashing lights and tickets. There were also no tables around it, either. No one was stupid enough to sit customers next to people throwing sharp objects.

"You are," I said. "Now throw them."

"Can't we just sit down and talk?"

"Look around," I said. "You see three guys having a quiet conversation anywhere in here?" I didn't wait for Donny to look and confirm what I said. "We blend in by blending in. Now, throw."

Donny put three darts into the board. The hits were all random and the points low. When he came back with his darts, he asked, "We keeping score?"

"No, Donny," Miles said. "We're planning a score."

"So you guys can, y'know, help me?"

"Depends on what you need help with," I said.

Donny looked around the room. When he saw that no one gave one shit about what we were saying, he said, "I need you to rob my store."

"We can do that. Did Jake tell you what we need?"

The little man nodded. "Sure. You're after uncut stones. I have some of those in my safe, but you'll need to take more than that. You need to clean me out."

I threw three darts and retrieved them. When I got back to the line, Donny said, "It can't look like an inside job. It can't. Alright?"

"We get that," Miles said. "Now throw your darts while you tell us about the place."

Donny looked at his hand. "Oh, yeah. Right."

We kept the darts moving while Donny gave us a detailed rundown of the store and its day-to-day operations.

"You gotta do it when I'm not around. I can't be anywhere near this. Do you understand?"

Miles and I nodded, but it was purely for show. There was no way we were going to let anyone else call the shots.

"Why are you so worried about getting fingered as the inside man?" Miles asked. "You dirty, Donny?"

Donny thought this was funny. "I'm here playing darts and arranging for two men to rob me. I'd say it's pretty evident that I'm dirty."

Miles chuckled. "You always been dirty, Donny?"

Donny looked at his scuffed leather shoes. "The business ain't what it used to be. In the eighties, I had the touch. These hands," he held up ten stubby fingers, "could craft art. People lined up for it."

"What happened?"

Donny shrugged. "I got cocky and set out on my own. I was doing well for a while, but I made some bad decisions and some worse enemies. You wouldn't think selling rings and bracelets would be a tough line of work, but there are some serious people doing this. I'm talking really bad guys. So anyway, things started going wrong at work, then at home. The wife walked out on me years back. I fought her tooth and nail for the business. I gave her way too much to keep it — way too much. I thought it was worth it at the time. Sure, the house and cars were money, but the business was a printing press. At least, that's what I'd thought."

"Things didn't work out?" Miles asked.

"I'm here, aren't I? I made some bad moves. I thought I could dig myself out, but I was wrong. I got in over my head with some people, and now I just want to get out. But I can't just walk away. I'm in the red everywhere, and I mean everywhere. I'm so stressed I'm shitting blood. Ulcers, y'know? So when I say I'm in the red, I really mean it."

"Yuck," Miles said.

Donny walked to the board and pulled the darts. "I've been telling people that I'm planning a comeback. I was going to launch a new line of original pieces that were going to put me back on the map. Except —"

"You're cashing out and not coming back," I said.

He pointed at me with one of the darts. "You got it. I've got plenty I can move when everything cools off. I've been buying a lot of uncut stones. Nothing fancy, but that's how I want it."

"Rocks beat paper," I said.

Donny smiled at me. He was happy someone under-stood him. "Every damn time. The stones are lower quality, so they won't set off anyone's radar."

"Like moving smaller denominations instead of hun-dreds," I said.

Donny winked at me. "You got it. It'll take a bit more time to move them, but if you know people, you can get a fair price. You'll get a fair price, too. You clean the place out and a cut of those stones goes to you. The rest comes back to me through Jake."

"Plus the insurance money," Miles said.

He jabbed the dart towards Miles. "That's right, kid. But don't get greedy. I'm giving you an easy score. I don't owe you a piece of the insurance for that."

I wasn't interested in hearing about cashing in on the insurance; I was more interested in something else Donny said. "You need to move those stones when the cops aren't looking at you anymore. Do you have a fence lined up?"

Donny tilted his head. "Why?"

"We're looking for a fence. Someone who can move some serious items."

Donny laughed as though he had heard a really good joke. He put an elbow on the table and leaned against it casually. The unsure, uncomfortable jeweller who was in over his head was gone; in his place was someone much more calculating. "And you want me to connect you with my guy? Why the hell would I do something like that?"

"The same reason you're here right now. There's money in it."

Donny used the tip of a dart to clean a fingernail. "I'm

not just going to give you a name. My guy wouldn't talk to you. He doesn't like doing dark business in the company of strangers. Remember those uncut stones I told you I've been buying up? My guy got me into that. He's been doing that for years, except he doesn't use his stones to make earrings; he uses them to help thick-necked Russians quietly move their drug money overseas under the noses of any government agencies looking to put an end to organized crime. See, my guy is a major player, and that means any deal with him will need to be brokered by me. And if I'm brokering the deal, then I get a percentage."

I stared at Donny and he returned the look with no sign of being intimidated. He had spent a lifetime in the diamond trade; he was a pro at making deals with hard men who were interested in pretty things.

"Your percentage comes out of the fence's cut, not ours."

Donny smiled and turned towards the dartboard. "I am sure it's something that can be negotiated."

"That's something that can happen after our business is finished. What time do you leave work tomorrow?"

"Tomorrow?" Donny's dart missed the board. "You want to do it that quickly?"

I nodded. "You leave at?"

"Five," he said.

"And the store closes at?"

"Nine."

"So we have a four-hour window. We'll hit the store around six. Who has the combination to the safe?"

"Tristan is the assistant manager. He knows the combination."

"I'll take him to the back room to open the safe. Ripley will work the floor and get everything on display. How many employees out front?"

"Tomorrow there will be two, but if business is slow I can send one of them home."

"You do that often?" Miles asked.

"From time to time."

"This time, don't. Anything out of the ordinary will put a spotlight on you, and you don't want that."

"No," Donny agreed. "I don't. That can't happen."

We played another couple games and picked the jeweller's brain. I brought up the fence again, but Donny wouldn't budge on the name. He insisted on being the intermediary to secure his cut. We sent Donny home when we ran out of questions. Miles and I stayed behind and found a pool table with a rare vacancy. We played a slow game of eight ball and drank on Jake's tab. Miles chose off the top shelf; I had coffee.

"You serious about using his fence?"

I lined up a shot and rammed the cue ball hard into a solid blue ball and watched it roll into the pocket. "Depends on Donny."

"You think that little shit will get us an honest deal?"

"I think it can be arranged."

"You have a plan don't you?"

I nodded and used the rail to sink another ball into a pocket on the other side of the table. "We can worry about Donny after we get our stones."

"We bringing in Monica on this?" Miles asked. He did a pretty good job of hiding his interest.

"Get in touch with her and tell her to be ready for four."

"Four? Donny said he didn't walk out until five."

I grinned and sank another ball.

CHAPTER TWENTY-SEVEN

At 4:44, Monica pulled to a stop in front of a fire hydrant down the street from Donny's Diamonds. She lifted her arm and pulled up her sleeve so that we could both see the old Timex Ironman watch on her wrist. "Seven minutes," she said. "After that, you're on your own."

"Some getaway driver," Miles said.

Monica turned around in her seat to look at Miles. "You're goddamn right I'm some getaway driver. You know why? 'Cause I get away. You want to get away, too? Get out here in seven minutes or less."

Miles opened his mouth, but Monica shut it for him. "Don't give me some smart remark, Miles. I do what I have to do. Always. No compromise."

I lifted my sleeve and entered seven minutes on my watch. "Seven minutes is fine."

I opened the door and the sound of traffic poured into the car. I got out and waited for Miles to meet up with me on the sidewalk. We were in front of an out-of-business dry cleaner two storefronts away from Donny's Diamonds.

Donny's store was nowhere near Mendelson's. The cab fare to get to the diamond district would likely get me one of Donny's higher-end pieces.

"What the hell was that?" he said.

I looked at the con man. "The hell was you, Miles. You expected our wheelman to be soft. Why? Because she's not a wheel*man*? She wouldn't be here if any part of her was soft."

"I think that might be why I like her so much."

I put a wool cap on my head and looked up and down the street; no one was giving either of us the time of day.

Miles moved beside me and chuckled while he put on his hat. He spoke under his breath while he did his own scan of the street. "We're robbing a jewellery store so that we can rob a jewellery store." He shook his head. "Nope, out loud it sounds just as crazy."

"David was more than just an inside man — he was our fence. That car accident killed our way in and our cash out. Donny gives us a second chance at both. With him we can get inside, and, more importantly, we can move the diamonds on the outside. We need him, and if robbing him gets him on board, then we stick him up."

Miles sighed and weighed my words. He looked at the scale; what came up made him shake his head in disapproval. "I don't care if both of you think rocks beat paper. This still seems crazy."

I checked the street one more time and then pulled down the cap. The hat doubled as a generic ski mask that mirrored dozens sold around the city. I looked at Miles and saw his eyes looking back at me from two holes in his mask.

We kept our heads down as we walked past the variety

store next to the jewellery store. At the door to Donny's Diamonds, I drew my pistol and entered the store with Miles at my heels. I went in with my gun in a two-handed grip. Two women screamed when they saw me and again when they saw Miles coming right at them. Miles corralled the two women into a corner while I moved towards the back rooms. I opened the door and went through it with my gun up. A woman stood on the other side of the door with a cup of coffee in her hand. One look at the gun and the mask sent a tremor up her arm and into the cup; it slipped from her grip and fell to the floor.

I advanced and took the woman by the upper arm and dragged her to the door I had just walked through.

"Incoming," I called to Miles.

"The more the merrier," he said before starting to whistle the tune to *Three's Company*.

I turned and walked to the office door Donny had described. Inside the office were Donny and Tristan. Tristan was shocked; Donny wore another kind of expression.

"What the hell is this?" Tristan demanded.

"Open the safe," I said.

"You won't get away with this," he said.

I shot Donny in the shoulder and pivoted the pistol so that Tristan could see the faint trail of smoke leaving the barrel.

"Open the safe," I said.

He nodded and pushed his way around the desk towards the large safe in the corner.

Donny moaned and the sound gained strength as it became a roar. "Fucking shot me!"

"That's what happens to innocent people in a robbery when people don't listen," I said.

"I'm so sorry, Donny," Tristan said. "It'll be okay. I promise."

Donny might have nodded, but it was hard to tell. Shock was setting in and draining his colour.

Tristan spun the safe dial one way and then another. "Shit."

He spun the dial a few times and started again.

I put the gun to the back of his head. "Slow down."

Tristan's hand froze. "Okay. Okay. It's just hard to do when my hands are shaking."

"Or you're trying to get in a few wrong combinations to engage a safety measure."

Tristan tensed. "What? No. No, I'm not doing that. I swear to God, I'm not doing that. I'm just nervous."

I took the gun away from the back of his head. "Take a breath."

Tristan pulled in a shaky lungful of air and let it out.

"Take a couple more."

He did.

"Better?"

"Yes."

"Good." I put the gun back to his head. "Do you know why I shot your boss?"

Tristan shook his head.

"I shot him to make things clear. I heard an expression once when I was inside. A guy said to me, *actions speak louder than words.* That action should be enough for you to understand who I am better than my first wife ever did.

Do you understand me?"

Tristan sobbed out the word, "Yes."

"Open the safe."

Violence and threats were tools I rarely employed if I could help it. More often than not, hurting people slowed things down instead of speeded them up. But I wanted the witness to the crime to walk away from the robbery feeling like he had dodged a bullet — literally dodged a bullet fired from the gun of an honest-to-God psycho. A psycho no one would think to connect to Donny. So I turned up the dial and talked just enough to leave Tristan with a story chock-full of vague go-nowhere details.

Tristan opened the safe without making another mistake.

I slid the bag off my shoulders and passed it to Tristan. "Everything into the bag."

Tristan busied himself while I checked my watch. We were coming up on four minutes. The assistant manager used the edge of his hand to wipe the contents of the safe into the bag. From over his shoulder, I could see that the diamonds inside the safe were nothing special. The stones were small and unimpressive; I imagined the police, and subsequent insurance claim, would see things differently.

"Faster," I said.

I glanced at Donny. His hand was over the seeping hole in his shoulder, but his eyes were on me.

"Fuck you," he said.

I pulled the bag away from Tristan and put it on my shoulder. "Your boss is bleeding profusely. My advice: keep pressure on it until the ambulance arrives. I'm talking serious pressure. You try to make a phone call with one hand and press on him with the other, he'll bleed out. Do the right thing. One of the ladies up front can make the 9-1-1 call when we leave."

I called to Miles as I walked through the door to the showroom. "We good?"

"Oh, sure," Miles said. He was leaning against one of the glass display cases. His bag was on top of the glass. The three employees weren't cowering in the corner; instead, they were on the opposite side of the cabinet leaning in towards Miles. Not one of the women looked distressed; one seemed unhappy to see me.

"That was fast," I said.

Miles smiled wide. "Turns out, Darlene, Emma, and Valentina don't care much for their boss. They were happy to help."

One of the women turned her head towards me. "You shoot him?" Her smile was devilish.

"Yeah, but don't get excited. He'll live."

"Time to go," Miles said. "Goodnight, ladies." Miles picked up the backpack and put it over one shoulder. "Do me a favour. Count to one hundred and then call the cops."

"We'll make it two hundred," the woman with the devilish smile said. "You said he won't die."

"Valentina, you are so bad," Miles said. "Have fun at your daughter's recital. I hope she remembers all of her solo. And if Hector doesn't show, don't let it ruin your time, or your daughter's."

"Thanks, Lando."

We stepped onto the sidewalk at six minutes and fifty-two seconds. Monica was waiting with her foot on the brake.

"Did she call you Lando?" I asked as I got into the back seat.

Miles smiled. "She most certainly did."

The car was moving before Miles had shut the door.

"Why?"

"Lando Calrissian is the smoothest criminal in the galaxy. I felt I could pull it off in the mask because you can't tell that I don't have a mustache."

Monica checked her mirrors and changed lanes. "I like a man with a mustache."

"Lose the mask, Miles."

Miles pulled off his ski mask and smiled wide. "So how did we do?"

"Went according to plan," I said.

"So you planned to shoot him?"

"Shit," Monica said. "We left a body?"

Her surprise didn't show in her driving. She kept the car moving with the pace of traffic using strategic lane changes and expert timing to slip through the traffic faster than everyone else.

"The body is breathing," I said.

"He was our inside man," Miles said. "He was on our side. Tell me why the hell you would shoot him?"

Monica took her eyes off the road and looked at me in the rear-view mirror.

"You worried about my judgment, Miles?"

Miles shrugged. "People seem to have a habit of getting

shot around you, and you are usually the one holding the gun."

What had gone down in Buffalo had never sat right with Miles. When we first met, the con man was still green and believed in ideas like honour among thieves. My beliefs were more primitive; I believed in an I for an I. When the Buffalo job went off the rails, Miles found himself a disciple in a land of nihilists. He had no choice but to follow me and bear the consequences of self-preservation at all costs; for some people, getting used to the weight takes time.

"He was greedy," I said.

"That's why you shot him?" Monica said.

"You might want to keep your eyes on the road instead of on me," I said.

"Don't worry about my job when we are talking about yours." Monica took the next corner without slowing down. Somehow, a glance was all she needed to thread through an opening between pedestrians. "You some kind of head case?"

"Am I, Miles?"

Miles thought about it. "No. No, I don't think you're a head case. But that opinion is getting harder and harder to defend every time you shoot someone."

"When did greed become a reason to shoot someone?" Monica said.

"When it threatens the job," I said.

"How did Donny threaten our job?" Miles asked.

"Double-dipping wasn't enough for Donny. He was looking at the insurance money and the fence on this job, and he still wanted a cut of our job. He's desperate, and desperate men make mistakes. Cops can spot greed, and they sure as hell can spot mistakes. We need Donny to make it past the cops so that he can fence our score. A bullet in his arm gives him a better shot."

"Was that a joke?" Miles asked.

"No."

Monica looked at me in the rear-view again. "You said we need Donny."

"We do."

"What are the chances he's going to need us after you shot him?"

"Good question," Miles said.

"I told you — he's greedy. He'll be mad, but it won't change anything. He only cares about the money."

Miles snorted. "I doubt that will smooth things over with Jake."

CHAPTER TWENTY-EIGHT

"**Y**ou want to tell me what the hell that was?" Jake was behind his desk, but he looked ready to come over it.

I pointed at the backpacks on the desk. "The job was the stones in the safe and everything else. It's all there. Less our cut."

Jake's face twisted into an ugly snarl. "You fucking shot your inside man. There's no rule book for what we do, but if there was, not shooting your inside man would be pretty close to the front cover."

"He was after his entire inventory, Jake. Not the pretty stuff or the real valuable stuff in the safe — he wanted everything. What are the cops going to make of that?"

Jake sighed and the anger that had been filling his sails dissipated. "They'd start with a hard look at Donny."

"And how long would it take them to see what I saw? How long would it take for them to see Donny for the greedy little shit that he is?"

Jake rubbed at the stubble on his chin. "That still doesn't give you the right to shoot him."

"You never said I was wrong about Donny."

"What? About him being a greedy little shit. News flash, Wilson, he's a criminal — we're all greedy little shits. That's why we don't have jobs."

"This is my job," I said. "And Donny is not like me. One thing drives him, and that thing would sell us out the second he's in a pinch."

"So you did this to keep our names out of it?" Jake rolled his eyes. "Maybe I should be thanking you instead of yelling at you."

"I didn't do this to keep Donny from squealing. I'm not worried about the law. Donny could tell the cops everything he knows about us and it wouldn't get them anywhere, but it would screw up the job. I need Donny out of a cell and on the street so he can get me what I need."

"I don't know if he's interested in providing anything to you anymore."

"What did he say?"

"He says you shot him and he wants his stones back."

I grinned. "If there were a rule book to what we do, do you know what would come before the part about not shooting the inside man?"

"What?"

"No refunds."

Jake rubbed at his chin again.

"Donny is being greedy again," I said. "Let him know where his greed will get him."

Jake sighed. "I'll see what I can do."

CHAPTER TWENTY-NINE

"They don't look like much," Monica said. She was wearing a white sweater with prefabricated holes in the arms. I caught Miles staring at the holes twice.

"They don't, do they?" Miles picked up a stone and tossed it into the air.

They were right. The small uncut diamond that landed in his palm didn't look like much, but it didn't need to.

"Have you ever seen an uncut diamond before?" I asked.

"Besides these? No."

Monica said, "Nuh-unh."

"The difference between the most and least expensive is difficult to determine if you don't have the expertise."

"And the thieves who are going to hit Saul's place aren't experts are they?" Miles said.

"Not according to the police," I said.

"There aren't exactly a lot of diamonds here."

"According to David, Saul's personal safe has uncut diamonds in it. He said the only one who knows what is in there is Saul. That means the thieves can't know, either.

They'll take what they find and assume the small number of stones means they're high quality and worth a large amount of money."

"But our thieves are supposed to work inside the store right?" Monica said. "Won't they be after all of the jewellery in the cases?"

Miles laughed and fished into a pocket of his jeans and came out with a diamond ring. "You mean jewellery like this?"

Monica's eyes widened at the sight of the ring.

"I didn't want to ask you with Wilson here, but will you marry me, Monica?"

She extended her finger and said, "No."

Miles chuckled and slid the ring on her finger.

"Where did you get this?"

"It's New York City and I'm a con man. Finding fake diamonds is not exactly an impossible feat. I used the pictures David gave us to get these made. They're cubic zirconia and not really that close to what's in Mendelson's display cases, but they'll pass just fine in a robbery in the dark."

"It looks real," Monica said.

"I know. I ordered an extra of that one. I got plans for that thing."

Monica took it off and handed it back to Miles. "I don't want to know. So why go to the trouble of getting the real stuff? Why not just use fake all the way?"

"Saul's on our side right now, but soon we're going to ask him to make a hell of a leap of faith. Jumping will be a hell of a lot easier if he's convinced we're committed. If we tell him that those diamonds came out of police evidence and that we are willing to risk using them in the sting, he'll take us seriously. And that is what we need him to do."

Monica nodded. "But are we just expecting Saul to let somebody break open his safes? Those things are expensive. He won't go for that."

Miles laughed again. "The risk is worth it. To Saul, this is about more than money — it's about getting justice for David. And speaking of David, don't forget he told the police that our thieves are technical wizards who can open the safes without leaving a trace, so Saul really has nothing to worry about."

"But we need him worried," I said, looking at Monica. "How did the tail go last night?"

Monica picked at what was left of her hamburger until she found a pickle hiding between the remaining bun. She ate the pickle and spoke while she chewed. "I kept back most of the way home, but I made it real obvious when we got close to his place. He saw me and panicked. He sped up and took a corner without stopping at the stop sign."

"You spooked him," I said. "He left a message on my phone around nine."

"That must have been just after he got home," Monica said.

"We'll pay him a visit tomorrow morning."

"Detectives Lock and Croft on the case," Miles said.

CHAPTER THIRTY

We were waiting for Saul outside of his parking garage. "Mr. Mendelson," I said.

He stopped in his tracks and lifted a hand towards the inside of his coat. "Who wants to know?"

"Sir," Miles said. "We're the police. We spoke the other day. Do you remember?"

Saul's eyes hardened. "Of course I remember. You're detective Lock," he said. "The other one is Croft."

"Actually," Miles said, "I'm detective Croft."

"That's what I said."

Miles smiled. "Of course. Sorry, sir. I haven't had my coffee yet. I'm still in a fog."

Saul pointed a finger at me. "I called that number you gave me and you didn't pick up. You show up, tell me someone murdered David, tell me my store is going to be robbed, and then you don't answer your phone. What kind of policeman are you?"

"I'm sorry, Mr. Mendelson. We were interviewing a suspect last night. It took all night. I just got the message a few hours ago and I thought it best that we come to you in person."

Saul clicked his tongue. "Likely story." He didn't remember our names, but he remembered that he didn't like me just fine.

"Why did you call?"

"Someone was following me last night. It wasn't the first time. The other day the same blue car followed me home. I thought it was a little strange the first time, but the car didn't stay with me, so I didn't really think anything of it." His eyes went wide. "Then, last night, the blue car was back. It followed me home."

I opened my pad and began scribbling notes. "Did you get the license plate?"

Saul glared at me. "License plate. Did you hear me? I was trying to get away from the car. I didn't have time to read the plate."

"Sorry, sir, I had to ask. It's procedure."

"You said it was a blue car?" Miles asked.

"Yes, that's what I said. I think I saw it again this morning."

"You think?" I asked.

"You think I'm making this up?"

I knew he was. Monica hadn't followed Saul this morning. David had told us that the old man suffered from paranoia. The blue car that he saw this morning was just something his mind fixated on and attached meaning to.

Miles stepped in front of me and entered Saul's personal space. "They're likely trying to find a pattern to your movements."

"Arrest them," Saul yelled.

Some people on the sidewalk turned to look at us. I put up my hands and shrugged in a gesture that said, *what can you do?* The gesture seemed to please most of the people who had looked at us. I guessed that they had elderly people in their own lives who yelled at them on the street.

"We will," I said. "But, not yet."

"Why the hell not?"

Miles put a hand on my shoulder and moved me back a few steps. When he turned to Saul, his voice was calm. "You know why, Saul. We don't want to bust these guys for stalking you. We want them for David's murder, and the only way we are going to get them for that is if we think big."

"So I'm just supposed to let them follow me."

"Yes," Miles said. "But I promise you won't be in any danger. We're going to assign a security detail to you. They will stay close enough to you to make sure that no harm comes to you. They will also do a little tailing of their own. If these guys show up again, we will follow them and find out everything we can about who they are."

Saul smiled. "Alright. I can live with that."

"Good," Miles said. "I know how stressful this is for you, sir, but it will be all over soon."

"How can you be sure of that?"

"If they're tailing you, they must be getting ready to do the job. That means we need to be ready for them."

"Oh, I'm ready for them. After what they did to my poor David, it's all I can think about."

"Make sure to stick to your schedule," I said.

The old man jabbed a finger into my chest. "I'll do my job. You just make sure you do yours."

"Great," Miles said. "We'll take the first shift tonight when you leave. Don't look around for us. Just drive home the way you do every night."

Saul smiled at Miles. "No problem, Detective."

CHAPTER THIRTY-ONE

That night, we sat inside our faux police car a block from Saul's Long Island home. He lived upscale, and the car stood out. The obvious modifications that gave the car the impression of being a law-enforcement vehicle kept the residents from calling the real cops. All of the dog-walkers who passed the car gave us pleasant nods; some even waved. The wealthy loved and trusted the law as much as the poor disliked and distrusted them.

"What time you got?" Miles asked.

"The same as you," I said.

"My watch says Saul is late."

I nodded.

"We told him to take the usual way home."

"We did," I said. "Maybe he forgot."

"Did you get the feeling that today was an off-day? He wasn't the same sharp old guy. I don't think he even recognized us at first."

"He didn't."

"And he should have. I mean, it's not every day the

cops show up and tell you that you are the target of armed robbers."

"It jives with what David told us. Saul is forgetful and confused. He's also angry."

"Only at you," Miles said.

"I seemed to have touched a nerve."

"Oh, you definitely touched a nerve. I don't know what you did, but that old man hates your guts." Miles took a sip of coffee and made a noise in the back of his throat when he realized it was cold. He put the cup back in the cup holder and went into his pocket for gum. "Maybe there was traffic."

I turned the key in the ignition and found a news station on the AM dial. We were nine away from traffic and weather on the tens.

"I'm going to call her," Miles said. He punched her number into one of the burner phones I picked up the week before. Monica had a matching phone, but she wasn't picking it up.

"We can rule out traffic," I said.

"Why?"

"If there was traffic, she would be able to pick up her phone."

Miles frowned. "So where are they?"

I pointed. "There."

Saul's BMW braked at the stop sign for the appropriate two seconds and stayed there for an unnecessary thirty.

"What's he doing?"

"He's looking for us," I said.

"We said we'd be watching."

"Maybe he didn't believe us." I flashed the headlights a few times and the BMW responded by turning in our direction. Saul eased to a stop next to our car and rolled down the window.

"Glad you changed your mind," he said.

"Thought you might be," Miles said without missing a beat. "What did you see?"

Saul laughed. "The blue four-door was following me again. I did what you said and kept driving as though nothing was happening. Your guys got it just before we got on the on-ramp."

Miles leaned across my seat so that he could get closer to Saul and his story. "How'd it go down?"

"A car — it didn't look like a police car, but I imagine that is the point — boxed the blue car against the curb. That was all I saw; I was getting onto the freeway."

"We saw how worried you were, so we decided to act," Miles said.

"But what about what you said? Won't this tip them off? I don't want them to get away — not before they pay for what they did to David."

"Don't worry," I said. "The traffic stop will be a case of mistaken identity. The cops who pulled over the car will let whoever was inside walk, but not before they get their identification."

"By tonight, we'll have everything we need on the car and whoever was driving it. You'll be safe now, sir; they won't want to risk tailing you again after this. We're hoping this will push things forward, so we need you to be ready to move when the time is right."

"I know what I have to do," Saul said. "You don't have to keep telling me that."

"We'll be in touch, sir," Miles said.

Saul nodded and said, "Alright," before rolling up his window and driving away.

"You think it was the cops? Maybe the plates weren't as clean as she said they were."

I thought about it. "It wasn't the cops."

"How can you know that?"

"When Saul told you about what happened, did he mention lights or sirens?"

Miles was uncharacteristically quiet. When he finally spoke, his voice had lost all trace of confidence. "If it wasn't the cops, who was it?"

"I don't know. But if they took her, I know where they're going next."

CHAPTER THIRTY-TWO

The drive back to the motel took an hour longer than it should have. Thirty minutes went into retracing our steps in search of Monica's car — it was gone. The remaining half hour went towards finding another ride. We found a rusted white Ford Econoline van parked on a side street and boosted it. Miles drove the van back to the motel parking lot and waited. He put in fifteen minutes of surveillance and then called me to tell me that there wasn't anyone waiting around.

I drove the fake police car back to the motel and parked it on a street a block away. I walked to Miles and got inside the van. The van belonged to a dedicated smoker intent on pushing the ashtray to its limits. The seats were torn where they weren't stained, and the rear compartment was picked clean of anything that didn't come directly from the factory.

Miles had been trying Monica's phone every fifteen minutes without success. The unanswered calls had him on edge. "What do you think happened to her?"

It was the seventh time he had asked the question; I gave him the seventh, "I don't know."

I had no idea what happened to Monica, but I was sure the motel room was burned. It didn't matter if Monica came back today, tomorrow, or never — the motel was no longer clean.

"How much longer are we going to stay here?"

"Another hour," I said.

"Then what? We just call it and move on? We need to find out who took her and get her back."

I gave it some thought. The timing bothered me. We were closing in on the job and one of our crew suddenly gets pulled off the street. It could have been the cops — maybe Monica ran afoul with one of the few cops who gave a damn about traffic violations or maybe she did something the cops couldn't ignore, like hit a pedestrian. It was possible, but not likely; she was a professional driver and that kind of bad luck didn't happen to really good drivers. Ruling out bad luck, that left bad intentions. Someone found her and snatched her because they knew what she was doing. But whoever did it doesn't know everything — at least not yet. If they knew everything, they would have just killed her on the street. They took her because they wanted information about the job.

"Did you hear me?"

I didn't answer because I didn't have one yet. If someone took Monica to learn about the job, the job was off. Monica knew everything and that knowledge was more than enough to make us easy pickings for someone looking to take the take.

"She's part of our crew," Miles said. "We can't just sit here, waiting. We should start with Saul. He has to know more about what happened."

I nodded. "We're not just waiting on her; we're waiting on whoever might be inside. We'll give it the rest of the hour and then we'll take our chances and go in for the gear."

"And then Saul," Miles said.

"Yes."

"He must know more than he told us," Miles said.

"We're not going back for answers," I said.

"What? If we're not after answers, then why the hell are we going back?"

I turned my head and looked at Miles. I had his full attention.

"We're going back because the job is tomorrow."

CHAPTER THIRTY-THREE

I laid out everything I had been thinking.

"So you think someone did this to get to us."

"Not us . . . the job."

"And you want to do it anyway."

"We lost our driver and it's too late to find a new wheel-man. But if we move fast, we don't need to. Saul saw her today, and he saw her go down — we can use that. We need to spin what he saw to our advantage. We'll tell him that we found out the job is happening sooner than we thought. That gives us another advantage. Monica thought we had another week before the job — whoever took her will think the same thing. Doing the job tomorrow will make whatever Monica gives up useless."

"Jesus Christ, you are an asshole. Do you hear yourself? I'm serious. Do you hear what you are saying? You don't care about her at all, do you? I knew you were cold, but —"

I stopped listening to Miles. Something else had stolen my attention. I put up a hand to shut Miles up. He swatted it away. I brought my hand up again, but this time I didn't try to silence Miles; instead, I pointed to the parking lot entrance.

Miles looked out the windshield. "Is that —"

I nodded.

A blue four-door had just pulled in and was headed our way.

CHAPTER THIRTY-FOUR

"**H**oly shit," Miles said as he went for the handle of the van door.

I grabbed a fistful of the con man's shirt and pulled him away from the door before he could push it open.

"Wait," I said.

"Wilson, that's her."

"Call her phone."

Miles started to argue, but I cut him off. "Call her phone."

He dug out the burner and dialled the matching unit; he got no answer.

"Doesn't mean anything. It could be off. It could have died."

"It's her car, but it might not be her," I said. "Wait."

This time, Miles didn't put up a fight. Together we watched the blue four-door pull up to the motel room and park in the centre of two spaces. The car idled, headlights on, for a full minute. The lights stayed on while the driver turned off the engine and opened the door.

Monica got out of the car on shaky legs and walked, doubled over, to the motel room door.

Miles said, "She's hurt. Let's go."

"Wait," I said.

"Wait? She's alone and she's hurt."

Monica rested a forearm on the door to keep upright and knocked. I quickly checked the street and then focused on Monica as she knocked again. I wanted to see what happened when the second knock didn't work.

Monica leaned against the door, her breathing laboured, waiting to be let inside. When nothing happened, she didn't look back at the car; she steadied herself with two hands on the door and then gave up on standing and sank to her knees.

Miles lurched for the door. I grabbed him by the shirt front before he pulled the handle. "Wait."

"She's fucking dying. What are we waiting for?"

"To see if anyone else is," I said.

No other cars had come into the lot or stopped on the street, so anyone watching Monica had either gotten there before she did or rode in the car with her. Putting someone in the motel ahead of time would have meant leaving Monica to drive there on her own; that was too much control to give a hostage — the car was the more likely place to keep a leash on Monica.

Monica fell sideways to the pavement in front of the motel room door. We did nothing and the parking lot did the same. Miles tried to move, but my hand around his throat kept him in the van. As one minute stretched to five, I watched the motel lot and listened to the soundtrack of angry curses and indignation playing from the seat next to me. No one came for Monica. I let go of Miles's neck and he exploded out of the Ford and sprinted across the parking lot. I walked behind him with a pistol in my hand. When Miles got within five feet of the brown motel door, I brought up the gun with two hands. I let Miles deal with Monica while I circled the car; there was no one inside. I went from the car to the motel door. I stood to Miles's side as he hovered over the body on the ground. With one hand, I fit the key into the lock and turned the handle. I butted Miles out of the way as I went into the room with my gun up. The living room and kitchen were empty. I went backward instead of forward and took hold of Monica's elbow.

A moan escaped the driver's lips.

"What the hell are you doing, man?" Miles barked.

I dragged the barely conscious woman into the room with Miles at her heels.

Inside, I let Monica down and closed the door behind her. Miles knelt beside her. "What is wrong with you?"

"Get your gun up," I said.

I stepped over Monica and crossed the living room. "Miles, take the bathroom." The con man nodded, went to the other door, and entered when I signalled. I timed my step across the threshold to the bedroom to match Miles's entry into the bathroom. Both rooms were empty — there was no one waiting for us — at least, not inside.

I checked the parking lot through the window before I checked on Monica.

"How is she?"

"Don't act like you care."

"Can she move?"

"Why, you gonna drag her again?"

I looked down at the woman lying at my feet. Someone had done a number on Monica's face and head, but my eyes didn't linger there. I used a finger to open the heavy army jacket she was wearing over a grey sweater. There was a large puncture wound low on her left side. The blood that had seeped into the fabric of her shirt and jacket was a wicked-looking black. It was a calculated wound. Someone had thought about where to stick her. The blows to her face that had split her lips and broken her nose were questioning wounds. Someone had wanted to know something. I put my gun down and lifted Monica's sweater. The hole in her side was round, but it wasn't a gunshot wound; the hole was neater than something a gun could produce. For a second, I wondered if someone had stabbed her because she wouldn't talk or because she had talked enough.

"Get some towels from the bathroom," I said.

"We need to get her to a hospital."

"Towels," I said.

Miles got up and went into the washroom. When he came back, I was at the window again.

"What's the plan?"

"Wipe down everything," I said.

"What? I thought you wanted the towels for her. We need to get Monica to a hospital."

I looked back at Monica. Something wasn't right; there was no symmetry to her wounds. They had battered her face and head with seemingly no focus, but then used a precision stab wound to leave her dying but mobile. The hole in her guts gave her time — time to run all the way back to us.

"We need to wipe down everything and get out of here. People are coming and we don't have much time."

"She's going to die on the floor if we don't do something."

I grabbed a towel from Miles's hands and went to work on the kitchen. He went back to the floor and put a towel on top of Monica's stomach. A minute later, I was in the living room working my way towards the bathroom. I finished the bathroom quickly and moved immediately to the bedroom. I didn't have to worry about the garbage cans; I had learned early on never to leave pocket litter lying around. I circled the final room and picked up the bags I had left packed and under the bed.

I put the bags down next to Miles and Monica and checked the parking lot.

"We are not leaving her." Miles's voice was low and serious.

Nothing in the motel lot had changed. It was like looking at a painting of rock-bottom America. It didn't make sense. The body was a trap — it had to be — so where was the hunter?

"You hear me? We are not leaving her here."

I ignored Miles and checked the lot again. The same cars were still in the same spots — nothing had changed. Then, something did.

CHAPTER THIRTY-FIVE

Red and blue lights strobed over the surface of the cars in the lot. The flashes quickened and the intensity of the light increased. In seconds it was no longer dark outside the door. The lights of the police car gave the motel a new electric sun twenty feet from the peephole.

I looked at Miles. "Do you still have your badge?"

The question pulled Miles's attention away from the driver. "Yeah, why?" Then, he noticed that the windows were glowing.

"Get it out."

"Why, Wilson?"

"It's Lock, Detective Croft. Someone just hurt our CI, and we just arrived on the scene."

I opened the door an inch and put my phone to my ear. "Keep pressure on the wound."

"Now you care?"

I peeked through the crack in the doorway and saw two cops getting out of the squad car. The driver was a woman and her partner was a man; both wore bulletproof vests and walked with hands on their guns.

When the two cops were five feet from the door, I yelled, "We're in here. We're in here."

The door was shoved open and the lead cop yelled, "Police," and pointed her gun at the three of us.

"Where's the fucking bus?" I yelled.

"Put your hands in the air," the second cop yelled.

"I don't have time for this, uni. Tell me where the fuck that fucking bus is."

"I said hands in the air."

I lifted my hand and showed them my badge. "Put that gun down and pick up your radio." I looked at the lead officer. "You, get outside and flag down the paramedics, goddamnit."

The cop didn't shout at us about our hands again. Instead, the other cop lowered her gun and took charge. "What is going on in here? We got a call about a possible assault."

"Change it to definite," Miles said. "This girl is our CI and she's dying on us."

"Wait," I said. "You said assault. We called this in. Didn't dispatch say anything about us being here?"

The cop looked at Monica, and I saw concern in her eyes. "We got nothing."

"Fuck! Okay, call it in again."

The cop turned to her partner and said, "Do it, Simmons."

The other cop had been staring at the pool of blood that had formed around Monica. He snapped out of it when he heard his name. He said, "On it," and went out to the car.

The other officer holstered her weapon and stepped closer to Miles and Monica. "What happened here?"

"Don't know. We were supposed to meet here, but when we showed up, the door was open and she was like this. It looks like whoever did this beat her up before they stabbed her."

"Explains the call about the assault," the cop said. "This her room?"

"Not sure," I said. "We've never met here before. She called my cell, told me she had something for me, and gave me a place and time. We rolled on it and found Tammy like this."

The cop kicked the duffel bags. "These her bags?"

"Not sure, either," I said.

"She going to make it?"

"If we get that bus in time," I said. "What's your name?"

"Garcia. My partner is Simmons."

I made a show of looking around the room. "Do me a favour, Garcia."

She looked around the room the same way I did. "Sure."

"See that bedroom over there?"

She looked at the room. When she turned her head back to me, it connected with my fist. The impact of the left hook didn't need the extra help from the cop's momentum to do the job, but it helped. The blow shut her down and her legs gave out.

Miles looked at the second body on the floor. "You got a plan here, Detective?"

"Count to thirty and then call for help."

I stepped outside and saw Simmons sitting in the driver's seat with the radio in his hand.

I let him see me. "Tell me that ambulance is close."

Simmons pulled the radio away from his mouth. "No one heard anything about an ambulance. I got one en route, but it'll be at least five minutes."

I nodded.

"I didn't get your name, sir. Dispatch wants to know."

"It's Lock," I said. "I'm a detective with homicide."

"Out of where?"

"We got an officer down," Miles called. "Officer down."

Simmons came off the seat and shouldered past me. "Garcia!"

I followed closely behind Simmons.

The cop knelt beside his partner. "What the hell happened?"

"She fainted," Miles said. "She a diabetic or something?"

I hit Simmons with the butt of my gun before he could answer. The blow caught him in the temple and sent his body on top of his partner.

I looked down at Miles. In the commotion, he hadn't moved an inch from Monica's side. "Pick her up."

CHAPTER THIRTY-SIX

I checked the lot before I opened the door again — there were no other additions. The squad car was in the centre of the lane, but it had stopped two spaces away from Monica's blue sedan. I turned to Miles, who already had Monica in his arms, and dug into her right coat pocket for the keys to the car.

I opened the door and motioned for Miles to step out first. He got one of Monica's feet out the door when a bullet shattered the door frame.

"Put — put her down." Garcia was on her side with a Glock in her hands that matched the one in my holster.

"Take it easy," Miles said.

"Shut up."

"We didn't do this to her. We just want to get her some help."

"Shut up and put her down," Garcia said.

"She needs a hospital, not the floor. Let us get her there."

Garcia blinked a few times and then shook her head back and forth to disperse whatever mental cobwebs had formed when she was out cold. "I'm not going to ask again."

I turned to Miles and slid two hands under Monica.

"What are you doing?"

"She needs medical attention. Officer Garcia is the best way to get it quickly."

Miles didn't let go of Monica until my pull elicited a moan from her broken lips. I took her weight out of Miles's arms and stepped back.

"Put her down. Do it now."

I nodded and pivoted my body. The one hundred eighty degree turn supplied momentum to my arms. When I had all the torque I was going to get, I released Monica's body and sent her tumbling across the space between us and the cop. From her position on the floor, Garcia couldn't risk shooting me out of fear of hitting Monica's airborne body. She decided too late to try to catch the body that was more than halfway to her. She scrambled to get up and get her arms out, but Monica hit her while she was still on one knee.

Miles and I reacted simultaneously. Miles went for Monica, and I went for my gun. I pulled the trigger twice and two bullets crossed the room before Garcia could get on two feet. The shots missed Monica and hit Garcia twice in the upper part of her vest before anyone could react to the noise. The sound was loud and the effect devastating. Garcia skidded back across the floor and collided with the coffee table behind her before rolling over to her side. She lay on the floor, eyes open, mouth making fish gasps for breath as her brain worked on autopilot to reinflate her lungs.

Miles got to his feet with Monica in his arms again. "What the hell was that? You could have hit her."

"Car," I said. I put the keys on top of Monica and went to Garcia. "I'll meet you there."

Miles turned and hustled Monica to the car. From my inner pocket I drew a knife. The blade sprang open and I took hold of Garcia's vest. I plunged the knife into the first bullet hole and used the blade to pry out the slug. I pocketed the slug then moved four inches to the left and did the same with the second hole. Garcia was still fish-mouthing as I walked out the door.

I took the wheel of Monica's car; Miles and Monica were in the back seat. I nosed around the police car and drove out of the lot without braking. I had no way of knowing if the cops got a good look at Monica's plates, but I wasn't about to give them a second chance. We transferred Monica to the unmarked car I had left a block away and drove west.

"What the hell just happened?"

"Whoever got hold of Monica is out to derail the job. They asked her some hard questions and then left her just alive enough to get back to us."

"And then they called the police."

I nodded and checked the rear-view.

"Why not just kill us?"

"Because it would be an unnecessary risk. We're not what they are after. They don't need us dead to get it. They just need us out of the picture."

In the rear-view, I saw that Miles hadn't taken his eyes off Monica. "They got a funny way of showing it."

"They're after the job."

Miles shook his head. "This was supposed to be an easy score."

"No such thing. If you thought there was, it's because you were telling yourself that."

"So who are we after?"

I hit the brakes and cut the wheel just as the cab in front of me cut into my lane without a hint of warning. I let the question hang in the air while I slipped into an opening in the lane beside me. I checked the rear-view and the side. "Doesn't matter," I said.

That got Miles to take his eyes off Monica. "How can you say it doesn't matter after everything that just went down?"

"Because it doesn't. I'm not a detective and I'm not going to waste any time pretending to be one. I know that someone is after the same thing we're after and they want us out of the way so that they can get it. That is what we deal with."

"And how do we do that?"

"We move on Saul tonight."

"Tonight?"

"Whoever is after us isn't shy. They're bold and they're smart. Our best defence is scoring and then taking our ball and going home."

"What about Monica?"

"Her part in this is over. We get her to a hospital and we walk away."

"We can't do that! The cops will pick her up in ten minutes. Those two uniforms saw her. They'll put a description out for a girl with her head bashed in and a hole in her side."

"Not in Jersey," I said.

Miles looked out the window at the traffic on the

interstate leading us west towards the Long Island Expressway. "Where we going?"

"Hoboken."

"They got cops there, too," Miles said.

"Her face looks like that because she wouldn't talk. I'm not worried about her handling the cops."

"She still gets her cut," Miles said.

"She still gets her cut," I agreed.

"You're an asshole."

Miles wanted to take Monica to the doors; I didn't try talking him out of it. I parked the car and reached back to turn off the overhead light before I got out to open the back door. In the darkness, the interior light would only bring attention we couldn't afford. Miles got out first and then stooped down to reach for Monica. I heard him grunt as he lifted her limp body from the car. When Miles had Monica out of the car, I said, "When you put her down, get a picture."

"A what?"

"A shot of her on the pavement. Use the flash."

"That's sick."

"Do it," I said before I got behind the wheel and closed the door.

Miles cradled Monica in his arms as he walked her away from the car. He set her down outside the entrance of the emergency room and took a picture of her body on the pavement; he also refused to talk to me the whole way out to Long Island.

I pulled to the curb across from Saul's house and dialled the number for his cell. I thought, given the late hour, I would have to let it ring. He picked up on the third.

"Did you get the guy?"

"Girl, actually," I said.

"Girl?" Saul's voice was thick with sleep, and he croaked the word out before he satisfied the urge to clear his throat.

"It's something we need to talk about."

"Okay."

"Now," I said.

"Now?"

"We're in the street."

Five minutes later, Saul was standing next to our car. He was wearing his blue coat, but he didn't have it open this time. He wore it buttoned tight over his thin pyjamas.

"It was really a woman in that car?"

"That surprise you?"

Saul looked at me as though I were a stupid child and he was out of patience. "Yes," he said. "It does. Now, who was she?"

"Her name is Amina Yousif," I said.

"Yousif?" Saul said.

The name had all of the impact I hoped it would.

"Sudanese immigrant. Records indicate that she immigrated to Canada five years ago," Miles said. On the drive over, he was silent, so I did the talking. I laid out the story and what needed to be said. I didn't micromanage — I knew Miles would be able to spin the details into a web that would hold Saul's trust. "Want to take a guess about the name of her closest relative in the States?"

"Ismail."

"You got it. Your security guard, Ismail Yousif, is her cousin. What does Ismail do for you, Saul?"

"He is in charge of my electronic surveillance. I can't believe what I'm hearing. Ismail?"

"It gets better," I said.

"Meaning it gets worse," Miles said. "Mr. Mendelson, we've learned some things. Ismail has been planning to rob your store for a long, long time. This plan has been in the works for almost as long as he has been in your employ. Over time, he has been working to circumvent your security system, so that he can get into the store at night."

"Impossible, we have alarms. I set them myself."

Miles interrupted Saul. "Ismail found a way around the alarm. He is actually quite an accomplished hacker. But those skills don't transfer to safe-cracking. That's where Amina comes into the picture. I don't know how much you know about Sudan, but it's not all war-torn. More than half the population is in their twenties, and there is a large network of organized crime. Ismail reached out to his cousin, who still has ties to the right wrong kind of people back home, and she convinced a crew to fly across the ocean. It would take a hell of a big score to convince people to cross continents. Word is the crew has everything they need in place for the job."

"What are they waiting for?" Saul asked.

"The crew was waiting on Amina."

"The girl? What did she have to do?"

"Just one thing," Miles said. "She had to kill you."

CHAPTER THIRTY-SEVEN

"**K**ill me?"

"Amina had been working in a hospital, and she managed to get her hands on a drug that would induce a heart attack. She was following you home because she was looking for an opening to inject you with the drug. The crew is ready to move as soon as they get the text."

"My God."

"You were supposed to meet him soon," Miles said.

Saul laughed. "But you arrested her."

Miles sucked in air through his teeth. "About that —"

Saul exploded. "You aren't going to tell me that she got away are you? She wanted to murder me for God's sake."

"No," Miles said. "She didn't get away." Miles pulled his phone out of his pocket and spent a few seconds pressing buttons. The burner was by no means high-tech, and it took some effort to get it to do what he wanted. Miles turned the phone and extended his arm towards Saul.

He looked at the picture and then at Miles. "Is she —"

"Yes," I said.

Saul took a step back from me as though I gave off a stench he could no longer tolerate. "You killed her."

"You saw the police pull her over, but you got on the freeway before you saw what happened next. Turns out, Amina was no slouch behind the wheel. She managed to get away from the men who pulled her over, and in the ensuing pursuit, she ran a red light and her car was struck by a cab driving through the intersection. We were not involved in the chase, but we weren't far behind."

"You being not far behind a woman out to kill me doesn't exactly fill me with confidence, Detective."

Miles took advantage of the short silence that followed Saul's jab to reinsert himself in the conversation again. "We were on the scene seconds after the accident took place. Amina was still conscious. That's how we were able to learn about the plot on your life."

Saul shook his head. "Such a young girl. I can't help but feel bad for Ismail." The old man laughed. "Isn't that silly? Ismail is trying to have me killed, so that he can rob my store, and I'm standing here in my coat and pyjamas feeling sorry for him." Saul shook his head again. "I don't know how I'm going to pretend I don't know about all of this tomorrow."

"About that," I said.

Deep lines formed between Saul's eyebrows as he trained his eyes on mine; he wasn't happy.

"What about *that*?"

Miles took over again. "We're going to need you to take the day off."

"Day off? I haven't taken a day off in forty years."

"I understand that —"

Saul cut him off. "Forty years. I've gone to work with pneumonia, bronchitis, shingles. I've been on death's door and still made it to work on time."

"Do you remember where he lived?" Miles asked.

"Who?"

"Death," Miles said. "Because we need you to find his place again."

CHAPTER THIRTY-EIGHT

Miles had been the one talking, but I was the one getting the feedback. "So now you want me dead, too? Tell me, who the fuck doesn't want me dead?"

Miles put up his hands and diverted the river of anger that had been rushing at me. I eased myself back a few inches, and Miles read the sign correctly. "Hear *us* out," Miles said as he took control of the conversation. "The plan was for Amina to kill you and then get to the border and her family in Canada. On the way out of the city, she had planned to message Ismail to tell him that you were dead. With you dead, Ismail and his crew would immediately hit the store and take everything inside. Amina said something about leaving evidence behind that you had robbed your own store before you died, but we didn't have time to get the whole story out of her."

"My God."

"We did get something, though."

"What?"

"We got the text she was supposed to send. She gave up the number and what she was supposed to tell Ismail to let him know you were dead. With you *dead*, we can send the text to Ismail."

"What? And let him rob my store?" Saul bellowed. "My store?" His voice carried down the empty street and woke a sleeping dog. A series of angry barks and snarls let us know how the dog felt about the noise.

Miles put his hand on Saul's shoulder in an attempt to calm him down. "Mr. Mendelson, I know what you're thinking. You're thinking, why don't we just arrest Ismail and end this?"

Saul shrugged the hand away. "You're damn right."

"All we have is the word of a dead woman," I said.

"And whose fault is that?"

"Ismail," Miles said. "It's his fault. Her death is on him, not us. You know who else he is responsible for killing?"

"Who?" Saul seemed genuinely unaware of the answer despite the fact that we had hung the responsibility for David's death on the security guard.

"David," Miles said. "He killed David. Remember?"

Saul, suddenly lucid again, waved a hand. "Of course I remember. David was like a son to me."

"The words of David and Amina — two dead people — aren't enough to arrest Ismail. We need more. We need to catch him in the act if we want to get him."

"How does that do anything for David?"

Miles didn't have a quick response. I had given him the broad strokes in the car, but he had been too mad at me to ask about the whole picture.

I took a step to the right so Saul could see my face; I could tell he wasn't thrilled about it. "Because we won't arrest just him. We are going to pick up his whole crew, and the first person who connects Ismail to David's murder gets to walk. Make no mistake, we are going to get Ismail for the robbery and for the murder."

"But not unless I help you by letting these thugs break into my store."

"You have nothing to worry about," Miles said. "Their whole plan hinges on there being no sign of a break-in. The store will be exactly as you left it."

"Except for the diamonds in my safe," Saul said.

Miles let his full smile loose. "We have that covered. Follow me."

Saul and I followed Miles to the trunk of the fake unmarked police sedan. He raised his hand in the air and I tossed him the keys. Miles popped the trunk and took a step back. "We've been working on this for a couple of days. We had to call in a couple of favours, but I think we did a pretty great job."

Saul stepped up to the bumper and looked inside. He squinted and then placed his hand on the rim of the trunk and bent down to look deeper inside. When he stood, he was holding a necklace.

"What the hell is this?"

"It's a necklace from your store," Miles said.

"No, it's not. There is nothing like this in my collection. Plus, it's fake."

"How can you tell?"

"That it isn't part of my collection?"

"That it's fake."

It was Miles's turn to get a dirty look from Saul. "Because it's obvious. You couldn't fool me with this."

"We don't need to fool *you*," I said. "We need to fool a security guard and some Sudanese criminals who are going to be emptying your two safes as fast as possible."

Saul dropped the necklace back into the case in the trunk. "It's crap." He went into the trunk and pulled out another piece. He gave the second necklace barely more than a glance before tossing it back into the trunk. "It's all crap."

Miles picked up the necklace and held it up in the streetlight. "It might not be a perfect match, but I would hardly call it crap. You think they're crap because you know what to look for. But Ismail isn't like you, he's like me. He'll see some shiny rocks and that will be enough for him. He's not going to check the stones. Why would he? They're in your safe. That will be enough for him." Miles let the necklace fall back into the case and turned his smile back on. "You haven't seen the best part yet."

Miles went into the trunk and pulled out a velvet bag. "Check these out."

Saul took the bag and reached inside. The stones he pulled out were small and yellow. He looked at them one by one in the streetlight and then walked to the driver's side door. Saul opened the door and turned on the headlights. The jeweller used the light to evaluate the diamonds.

"We had to raid the evidence lockers for those. You can't tell me they're fake," Miles said.

"No," Saul confirmed. "They're not. What they are is more crap. What the hell am I supposed to do with these?"

"They go in the safe in your office. We know that's where you keep your uncut stones."

"You do?"

Miles nodded.

Saul took the diamond away from the light and walked back to the driver's seat. He reached inside the cruiser and turned off the headlights. "How did you come to know about what was in my safe?"

"David, Saul," Miles said. "He didn't give us specific details, but he did mention uncut stones in your safe."

"He mentioned them?"

Miles nodded. "He believed they were one of the reasons the thieves were targeting you. I don't think I have to tell you how easy uncut stones are to move. But you know all of this already, Saul. We went over this the other day on the phone. We used your input to come up with this plan. Your ideas are what make this sting possible. We couldn't have done it without you."

I looked at Miles. There was never a phone conversation with Saul about any of this. There was never even a conversation with me about this. Miles was making a very dangerous play. I glanced at Saul and saw that he was staring at Miles, too. Miles was gambling on Saul's dementia; worse, he was gambling on Saul being aware of his dementia. Saul had been slipping for years and Miles was betting that he had developed a habit of covering his ignorance of his own actions by playing along as though he were up to speed on everything.

Three long seconds went by before Saul nodded. "I'm glad I could help."

"So you're still on board?" Miles asked.

Saul kept his eyes on the diamonds and fakes in the trunk while he thought about it. Everything had led to this moment and there was nothing left to do but wait. We had created a lie that placed Saul and his business in the centre of a fantastic tale of greed, revenge, and international intrigue. The story was far-fetched, but those were the kind that were the easiest to sell. It wasn't the details that would make the tale believable, it was the way it made Saul feel. The whole story put Saul at the centre of everything: an international gang of criminals was after him and the only way to stop them was for him to lead a police sting. It made Saul seem important, and that was good. People want to feel important more than they want sex or money; the success of our grift was dependent on how important it made Saul feel.

Saul picked up one of the real uncut diamonds we had taken off Donny. He held it up in the moonlight and shook his head. "No one who knows anything about diamonds will ever believe this is one of mine. But if this is the only way we can get them, well, then I'm on board."

CHAPTER THIRTY-NINE

Saul insisted on changing before we drove him to his store. We told him that we didn't have a lot of time, but there was no changing his mind. He also demanded to ride up front with us the whole way there. I said no, but Miles caved and gave up his seat.

Saul grumbled about our diamonds the whole way there while Miles lobbed excuses and apologies from the back seat. I was happy when we pulled to the curb in front of Mendelson's and was able to diffuse the argument with the words, "We're here."

Saul looked out the window and nodded. "Open the trunk and wait for me here."

"No," Miles said. "We'll come in with you. We can help you carry everything."

Saul turned his head to look over the seat. "Kid, I'm already letting one group of people look inside my safes tonight. I am not doing it twice."

Miles started to speak, but Saul cut him off.

"I don't care if you are the law. This is my business. Mine

alone. That means I do this myself."

I tried to make Saul see it our way, but he dismissed me with a wave of his hand. Miles tried to sweet-talk him, but Saul wouldn't budge. Eventually, Miles gave in and I had no choice but to play along. Saul took the diamonds and, with our help, wheeled the case up the stairs and into the store.

He told us it would take a few minutes — it had been ten when Miles said, "What do you think sold him on this?"

I looked at Miles leaning his back against the hood, and then I looked back at the store.

Miles kept on talking. "I think he feels a duty to David. He loved the kid. Love makes people do stupid things."

I looked at my watch. Eleven minutes. Miles caught my look. "He's been in there awhile."

"More than a few minutes," I said.

"He's an old man. It's late. Maybe he had to pee. I hear that's a thing with old men. Something to do with the prostate. You ever get yours checked?"

I glanced at my watch again.

Miles looked at his dick. "I'm thinking about it."

I got off the hood and walked around to the driver's side. At thirteen minutes, I opened the door and turned the key in the ignition.

Miles looked at the door to Mendelson's. "He coming out?"

Through the open door, I said, "Something is wrong." I put the car in drive and kept my food on the brake.

Miles opened his door and leaned in. "We are not leaving, not after everything that's happened. There are millions in there."

"Exactly," I said. "There are millions in *there*. We're out *here*, and unless Saul opens that door we are not getting near anything inside."

"What? You think he made us?"

I didn't know. I hadn't seen him flinch or any other sign that indicated Saul suddenly didn't trust us.

Miles got into the car but left his door open. "You know what's weird about Saul?"

Miles had my interest. "What?"

"David led us to believe that this guy needed help to eat his applesauce, but for an old, senile guy, he was incredibly hard to work. Usually, you can con the elderly into almost anything without breaking a sweat, but this guy — this guy made us earn every inch we got."

Miles was right. Saul had never once let us manipulate him blindly; we had to work to convince him to do everything. It wasn't even we — it had been Miles who had done most of the talking. Early on, Saul decided that he hated me as much as he liked Miles. We had rolled with it because we had no other choice. Something snagged in my head. A thought was there, but I wasn't sure what it was.

I looked at my watch — fifteen minutes.

I tugged on the line. "Why does he hate me?"

Miles laughed. "I didn't take you for a sensitive soul, Wilson. I don't know. Why do most people hate you? You're cold, you're mean, you shoot people you know . . ."

I tugged harder on the line and felt something coming. "But why does Saul hate *me*?"

"Who knows? Just thank your lucky stars that you were smart enough to bring me along. Saul liked me."

There was no reason that Saul should have hated me so much; at least, not one that I could decipher. I took a slow breath in. If I was right, and there was no reason why he should have hated me, then it was a conscious decision — a play.

"There's something I'm not seeing," I said.

"Jesus, do you hear yourself. He doesn't like you. That is nothing new. Sometimes, I don't like you." Miles slapped the dashboard. "You know what your problem is? You're not mad that he doesn't like you; you're just mad that you couldn't run everything. You can't handle letting anyone else call the shots."

Then, I got it. All of it.

"I call the shots?"

Miles threw up his hands. "I'm amazed you didn't pick out my underwear for this."

"It's that obvious."

Miles laughed. "It would take a real idiot not to notice."

"Do you think Saul is an idiot?"

"What are you talking about?"

"You let him go in there alone," I said.

Miles turned to face me. He raised his voice. "You're blaming this on me? Gee, I wonder why Saul doesn't like you more."

"Listen to what I am saying. *You* let him walk in there alone. You made that call. I wouldn't have."

"Fuck you. You are such an asshole. Do you know that? If you didn't like the way I played it, you should have said something."

"That's my point. Once you made the call, I couldn't say anything. It would have tipped Saul off."

"What are you saying?"

There were three possibilities; I laid them out for Miles. "One: Saul is taking his time switching the diamonds. Two: Saul made us tonight, and he's not coming out. Three: Saul's not coming out because he was on to us from the start and he's the one who is running the con."

The patrol car coming down the street eliminated option one and made the other choices momentarily irrelevant. Whether Saul made us tonight or two weeks ago didn't matter. It was time to leave.

Miles punched the dashboard. "Fucking diamonds and hitches."

CHAPTER FORTY

I took my foot off the brake and Miles pulled his foot inside.

"We're bailing?"

"We have company," I said.

Miles turned his head and saw the cop. "Shit. You think it was Saul?"

"Yes."

"Why no lights and sirens?"

As if on cue, the police car lit up and interrupted the dull hum of three a.m. in the city.

"I just had to say it," Miles said. "I just had to fucking say it."

I took a right at the first corner I saw and pulled to the side of the road. I was double-parked, but at three in the morning no one was going to complain about it.

"What are we doing?" Miles wasn't panicked; he just wanted to be on the same page.

I watched the rear-view as the cop pulled to a stop behind us. I could see him reach for the radio. Two hundred metres in front of me, the light was green.

"Is he getting out?" Miles was too smart to turn his head to look.

"No. He's running the plates and calling for backup."

"Shit."

The light went yellow, and I moved my foot to the right. The hard acceleration surprised Miles and he fought the pull towards the seat. "Holy shit."

"Buckle up," I said.

Miles got his seat belt on as the nose of the Ford entered the intersection. The cruiser was behind us, but it wasn't on our bumper yet. The cop's hands had been busy with whatever electronics were in his car and his mind was distracted when I hit the gas. We had gotten ahead of him, but it wasn't a race — the game was tag and we were it. I went right at the corner and heard the tires whine as they tried to find a solid grip on the road. I pushed the pedal hard to the floor and let the Ford get twenty metres up the wrong way of a one-way street before I again took advantage of the early morning traffic conditions. I hit the brakes and cut the wheel, sending the Ford into a tight aggressive U-turn. I was back on the gas the second I saw the stoplights of the intersection and drove the Ford back into the intersection just as the cop started to mimic my previous turn around the corner.

The cop saw us coming, but it was too late for him to do anything about it; he had committed to the turn and he had to see it out before he could turn around. I took a right at the intersection and fed the engine more gas. A street opened up on my left and I cut across the road and the car in the other lane to get to it.

New York streets were essentially a grid, and in the pre-dawn hours the traffic was light enough to allow me to weave through the grid at a speed faster than a jog. I kept the car moving in a zigzag and by the fourth turn, there was no longer any sign of the cop that had been chasing us.

"Pull over," Miles said. "We can ditch the car and walk away."

That had been my plan until a second police car turned out of a side street ahead of us. I gave the Ford some gas and gripped the wheel tighter while I waited for the cop to respond. The cop wasn't interested in a head-on collision, and he opted instead to let us pass and fall in behind us with lights and sirens.

"We're not going to outrun this one, Wilson." Miles reached into his coat and withdrew his pistol. "Not on our own, anyway."

"Put the gun away," I said.

"You serious?"

In the rear-view, I saw another cruiser swing onto the street and join the chase.

Miles turned to look out the rear window when he heard the duet of sirens. "Great, now there's two. Just great. Alright, new plan. I'm going to tell them you kidnapped me and made me do it. I'd be grateful if you played along."

I ignored Miles and kept tracking the streets.

"We're fucked," Miles said.

I likely would have agreed with the con man, especially after the third police car joined the pack that was getting close to nipping on our bumper, but we had just passed 33rd Street.

On 34th, I turned the wheel hand over hand without taking my foot off the gas. The tires squealed and the car flirted with letting two wheels do the driving, but the Ford managed to take the turn without tipping over. I shoved Miles off me and wove around a car following the rules of the road. Thirty-fourth wasn't empty at three thirty in the morning. There were enough cars on the road to turn our sprint into a slalom. I held no allegiance to the lanes while pushing the car faster and faster. Miles kept his head pointed towards the rear windshield.

"Whatever this is supposed to be, it isn't working."

"You're buckled, right?"

Miles took his eyes off the police cars behind us and looked at the strap across his chest. The word came out slowly. "Ye-ah." He angled his head so that he could see the speedometer. "What are you going to do?"

I saw the stairs on the left. These ones weren't like the others — they would work. I let the Ford drift into the left lane and made another car do the swerving for once.

"Tell me this is part of the plan."

I wasn't a driver. I didn't have the precision and finesse of a wheelman. I was competent behind the wheel, but I never had a knack for making cars do the kinds of things that made the laws of physics do a double take. I knew all of this as I paralleled the curb; I also knew my chances of shaking three cops on my bumper. I stopped thinking when I saw the green railings of the subway entrance — I gave up on thinking, clenched my teeth, and yanked the wheel to the left.

CHAPTER FORTY-ONE

The sharp change in direction and the nudge from the concrete curb took the car off of all four of its wheels. I had wanted to thread the needle and send the car down the stairs, but I wasn't a wheelman. The Ford stayed on its two left wheels for less than half a second and then opted for rolling over. The Ford rammed into the railing of the stairwell and lost its forward momentum in less than a second. The airbags exploded into existence with a loud bang as the green railing cleaved a jagged wound into the driver's side window. The rear section of the railing caught the Ford like a line drive to first and halted its momentum with a savage jolt.

"You alive?"

Miles groaned.

The seat belts had kept us in the car, but gravity was working at getting us out of our seats and down to the roof. "Yes or no, Miles."

"I'm alive," he croaked.

"Get your belt off," I said. "Don't fall on your head."

Miles rubbed his head. "What?"

"Belt."

"Oh, okay."

"Watch your —"

Miles released his seat belt and crashed into the ceiling. I was no doctor, but I took Miles's complete failure to react to the fall as a sign that not one hundred percent of him made it through the crash intact.

I put a hand on the roof and used the other to click the seat belt. I fell with less grace than a cat but with way more than the con man. I took the impact on my shoulder and quickly worked my legs under me. The windshield had taken a worse beating than my partner, and it took only a few kicks to make a hole big enough to crawl through. I slid out of the car, pulling Miles along behind me.

Miles put two feet on the concrete stairs and spent a few seconds figuring out how to navigate a world that was probably spinning a lot faster than he was used to. I started down the stairs and was pleased to see that he followed without being told. Any pleasure I felt disappeared when I got to the bottom of the stairs and saw Miles plodding four steps behind. It wasn't his speed that furrowed my brow — it was his right shoulder hanging out of its socket that had me concerned.

When Miles stepped off the stairs, I took hold of him with two hands and pivoted my body. The sudden movement put him against the wall and confused him enough to give me time to get my hands on his shoulder. In one movement, I jammed the bones back into place and then stepped back to let Miles deal with the pain.

He handled the additional pain louder than I thought he would have, and I had to brace him against the wall with my forearm against his windpipe to quiet him down.

"Shut up," I hissed.

Miles brought his hands up to my face and pressed his fingers into my eyes. I shook my head and pushed my mouth close to his ear.

"We don't have time for this. Now shut up and get your badge out."

I let Miles go and took out my badge.

Miles wheezed, "They know we're not cops."

I jutted a thumb towards the stairs and the smoke starting to snake out of the shadows and into the light. "They know we're not cops." I pointed in the direction of the terminal ahead of us. "They have no idea we aren't. We need to take advantage of that while we can."

I heard shouts coming our way. "In or out, Miles?"

Miles rubbed at his throat and then worked out the word, "In." It almost sounded like him.

I pulled my gun and kept it pointed at the floor. I looked at Miles and saw a glassy-eyed return of my gaze. It was the best I was going to get.

"Follow my lead," I said to Miles before I yelled out, "NYPD! Everyone get back! NYPD!" Badge up and gun down, I walked around the corner.

There were two people waiting for us. One was wearing a subway worker's uniform; the other wore the uniform of someone on professional twenty-four-hour street patrol.

I focused on the man with a job. "Are you in charge down here?"

"What?"

"Are you in charge down here?"

The middle-aged guy with grey on his temples and in just the middle of his moustache looked around. "Yeah, I guess. I mean, I work here."

"Then you're in charge. Get on your radio and relay a message to your supervisor."

"What the hell is going on?"

Miles beat me to the answer. His shoulder might have been wrecked and his bell might have been rung, but his mouth was fine. "Terrorists," he said. "They're using cars this time. Filling them with gasoline and fertilizer and then using them like Kamikazes. We need everyone away from the exits. Just get everyone into a washroom and stay there until we notify you that you can exit. Can you do that?"

The guy looked at our badges and guns and then at the smoke that had started to follow us. "I can do that, Officer."

"Detective," Miles said.

"Sorry, Detective." The subway worker turned to the only other person in the terminal. "Let's go. We need to get into the washroom."

"We're going back up. Make sure that you keep everyone down here safe."

The man stood up a little straighter. "I can do that, sir."

We watched the subway worker open the gate and usher the vagrant through. I gave them thirty seconds before I said, "Let's go."

I hopped the turnstile and helped Miles over. When we got to the platform, we found it empty. I crossed the platform to the mouth of the tunnel and climbed down onto the subway tracks.

Miles eased himself to the concrete and draped his legs over the side of the platform. He paused and let his legs dangle out of sight. "You sure this is a good idea?"

"No," I said. I didn't wait to see if Miles would follow me, and I didn't look back. If Miles had second thoughts about the getaway route, he could work it out with the cops who were currently figuring out a way around the smoking vehicle we had left in our wake.

The mounted fluorescent lights tinged the subway tunnel an eerie blue and created just enough ambient light to make the graffiti along the walls visible. We weren't the first people who had decided to use the tunnel as a footpath, not by a long shot. I jogged beside the tracks, listening for any sign of a train on its way towards me. It was late and there should have been less cars on the tracks, but I wasn't having any luck with things working out like they were supposed to.

As if on cue, I felt the faint rumbling through the soles of my shoes. The rumble climbed my legs as it became a sound. Ahead, I saw the tunnel illuminate as the train got closer. I considered hugging the wall, but I didn't want a driver to report two men in the tunnel. That report would go straight to the cops and put them back on my scent when I was no longer in possession of a combustion engine. I wasted a second looking over my shoulder for Miles and saw that he was trailing five metres behind me. There was a concrete divider twenty metres ahead of me where the track widened to accommodate some space that was previously used but now neglected. I yelled to Miles to move faster and started running.

The ground, uneven and littered with all manner of trash and debris, slowed me down, but the bend in the tunnel gave me an advantage. The train was approaching fast, but it wouldn't be able to see me or Miles until it came around the bend. I slid behind the divider and scrambled to the edge to look for Miles. The con man was lagging ten metres behind. He was having more trouble than I had with the uneven ground. His need to clutch his damaged shoulder didn't boost his speed, either. I didn't check on the train. The light in the tunnel and the noise in my ears told me that it was coming around the bend.

"Drop," I yelled.

Miles kept running.

"Get on the ground!"

Miles saw the train.

"Drop!"

He kept running. He fell behind the barrier a second before the train rolled past, and long after the driver got a good look at him.

The second the subway was out of sight, I said, "Go."

Miles was slow getting to his feet. I took him by his good arm and sped him up.

"How much time do you think we have before they figure out we're in the tunnel?"

"Less, now that the conductor saw you running beside the tracks."

Miles spoke around huffing breaths. "I should have dropped to my stomach."

I grunted a response and pulled Miles along a little faster. The tunnel was quiet after the train had passed, and I worried that the natural silence of the space made the clamour of our ragged breaths and the beat of our heavy feet stand out. I kept worrying as I ran. The only advantage we had came from the confusion created by the tunnels. The police had to cover two directions at once, and that kind of response took time to orchestrate. If we moved fast enough, we might have a chance of evading the net being thrown over us.

After ten minutes, the tunnel began to shed its darkness. Dim light from the next station was working its way towards us — and so were the focused beams of flashlights.

CHAPTER FORTY-TWO

"**S**hit," Miles said.

"I see them."

"I can't go back the other way. I don't have the steam for a chase."

"Can you climb onto the platform?"

Miles squinted down the tunnel. "I could do it, but it's not that simple. I see —" He paused to squint some more. "Two guys with flashlights coming towards us. You think they're cops?"

I moved away from the wall and looked down the tunnel. I saw orange vests instead of black. "MTA. Word about us escaping must not have reached the trains yet. He probably called us in as vagrants or urban explorers."

"Think we can badge them?"

I looked at Miles. His right arm was hanging loosely at his side and his head had an egg-sized lump near his temple that had swollen and become discoloured while we were running alongside the tracks. "We? No. No one is buying you as a cop looking like that."

"Looking like what? What do I look like?" He grabbed my arm. "What the hell do I look like?"

"Perfect," I said. I took hold of the back of his jacket and pushed him forward.

"What the hell are we doing?"

I spoke into Miles's ear, "I'm arresting you." Then I shouted to the men down the tunnel. "You two better not be my escorts."

"Stop right there." The voices were responding to what they had heard not what they had saw. The beams of their flashlights began a frantic search that ended when one of the lights flashed across Miles's face.

I kept my voice loud and full of the kind of authority that could only be gained by permission to carry a gun around. "I was told I was going to have two men help me search the tunnel. They also said that they would stop the train from coming through. I guess you guys are oh for fucking two."

Both lights were on Miles as we approached. Miles tucked his chin into his chest to avoid the blinding glare.

When the voice that had told us to stop barked at us again, it was ten metres away. "What the hell are you talking about? We got a report of two men walking on the tracks. They sent us down here to find out if it's true."

"That was me and this piece of shit right here."

"Hey," Miles complained.

"Shut up." I looked over Miles's shoulder at the two men while I erased the distance between us one step at a time. "He jumped off the platform and ran down the tunnel. I called it in. You telling me no one relayed the message?"

Up close, I could make out the two MTA workers. They were an odd pairing. Each man seemed to be a direct contrast of the other. The speaker's excessive body weight and four-day-old stubble looked slovenly next to the toned body and baby face of his partner. The bigger, older man was apparently the one in charge because he did all the talking. "No one told us anything. Like I said, we got word from the conductor that there was a man down in the tunnel."

"So you're down here to find him?"

"That's right."

"And now that you have?"

"We call it in and get you off the tracks."

"You have a radio?"

The fat man nodded. "Of course I got a radio."

I took the gun away from Miles's back and pointed it at the bigger of the two men. After some slow reaching, peppered with groans, Miles got his gun out, too.

"What the hell is going on?"

I stepped left so that the kid could see what kind of situation he was in without his partner's body blocking his view.

"Who do you call in to?" I asked.

"Our supervisor, Jimmy."

"Radio Jimmy right now and tell him you saw a man in the tunnel. You hear me? A man. Tell him you think he was a bum and that the guy went running back the way he came when he saw you."

The bigger of the two men looked at my gun before he looked at me again. "Listen, I got no problem with you. Walk away right now. We won't try to stop you. Just don't do nothin' stupid."

I kicked the man in groin with as much force as I could muster. He went to his knees and then onto his side. His mouth made wide silent gasps that pulled no air into his lungs.

I pointed the gun at the kid. "Radio Jimmy right now and tell him you saw a bum run back the way he came."

The kid said, "Okay. Sure, no problem." He pulled his radio from his belt and brought it to his mouth.

I took a step closer. "Stick to the script and everything will be fine."

"Okay." Before he used the radio, he looked at me and said, "Could you maybe point the gun someplace else?"

"No."

The kid nodded, took a shaky breath, and radioed his supervisor. Miles and I listened as he fed his boss the lines we gave him. Jimmy didn't like what he heard because it meant he had to make "a fucking hell of a lot of fucking calls." The kid replied with, "uh hunhs," until Jimmy got sick of talking and moved on to start his calls.

The kid let his radio dangle in his hand. "So now you'll let me go, right? I mean, that's our deal."

Miles laughed and then said, "Ow."

I pointed at the fat man on the ground. He was breathing again, but he wasn't trying to get to his feet. "His clothes. Now."

"What?"

"Get his clothes off, and then lose yours."

Five minutes later, we were dressed in coveralls, an orange vest, and a hard hat.

"Cops, now construction workers. I feel like I'm in the village people."

I ignored Miles and dragged the kid's unconscious body to the side of the tunnel where his partner was already laid out.

"Time to go."

"What's the plan?"

"We walk back to the platform, climb the stairs, and walk away from each other."

Miles nodded and followed behind me. "Y'know, I gotta say, I'm kind of surprised. I thought you'd shoot me or leave me in the tunnel because I was slowing you down. You might be going soft, Wilson."

Miles had watched me kill a man to get out of a jam, and the experience had left an impression. I didn't bother to tell him that the calculations that had led me to pull the trigger was the same cold math that had kept him alive. I had put up with the delays and complications of dragging the con man along with me because I had the endgame in mind. We were going to walk out of the tunnel and separate. The cops were looking for two men, so we'd split up and become something else. I could have left Miles behind and walked out alone, but I wanted the two of us to stick together; especially when one of us was Miles. He was hurt and moving slowly. That made him bait moving in the opposite direction.

CHAPTER FORTY-THREE

I got on the first bus I saw and rode the route until we passed a church. I got off at the next stop and doubled back. In the rear lot of the church was a clothing donation box that I had spotted as the bus rolled by. The box was full and people had left donations in garbage bags on the pavement. I pierced the first trash bag and wasted a minute sifting through women's clothing. The second bag had some men's items, but it was all beachwear. I finally scored on the fourth bag. Inside, I found jeans, a sweatshirt, and a coat that matched the season. I dumped the rest of the bag onto the pavement, changed, and packed the sweaty suit and coveralls I had worn over top of it into the bottom of the bag. I scooped up the spilled clothing on the pavement and refilled the bag before tying a new knot.

I left the bag in the pile and got on the next bus I saw. I let the bus be my getaway car and put a few miles and hours between me and Mendelson's. Eventually, I got off, found a cab, and went to LaGuardia. I walked the terminal until I found a crowd of people waiting on a delayed flight from London. There were numerous angry conversations taking place; some in person, but most of them over the phone. I stood on the periphery of the group and became just another member of the cellular herd. Saul answered on the second ring.

"Hello?" The old man's voice was confident; it wasn't the voice of a man who was scared for his life — or his property. The single word sounded more like a gloat than a greeting.

"I have a question," I said.

"Just one? I'd think you'd have a few more than that."

"Was it you who hurt the girl?"

The question caught him off guard. "I don't know what you're talking about." Saul sounded disappointed. He was like a magician dying for me to ask him how he did his trick.

I believed what he said. He wasn't responsible for what had happened to Monica. "You aren't who I thought you were," I said.

"You are exactly who I thought you were the whole time."

I let the insult slide. "I know you now," I said.

"What is that supposed to mean?"

I didn't answer. "I have one more question."

Saul laughed. "I'd say you earned one more for what you paid."

"Why did you kill David?"

The line went quiet and for a moment I thought Saul had hung up on me; then the old man cleared his throat and said, "Everyone wants to be king. The people who stay king never forget that." Saul sighed. "David spent too much time staring at the throne. He was so focused on the chair that he never considered the man on it might be staring right back at him. I saw him. I saw what he wanted. I loved the kid; don't ever think I didn't. I loved him enough to give him time to change his mind. But he didn't change his mind did he?"

Saul hung up before I could answer.

It had all gone wrong with David. He had come to us with a story about an old man ruining a business worth millions. David loved the man and he served him loyally until senility began erasing the man and the business' profits. It was a tragic story that we all bought into, but it was just that — a story. Everything that David had told us had been bullshit. Everything except the payoff — the diamonds were real.

I walked away from the crowd of frustrated family and friends still waiting on the plane from London. I pulled the SIM card out of the phone and dropped both into the first garbage can I passed. I checked the boards and saw that the flight I wanted wouldn't be leaving for a couple of hours. I bought my ticket and then found a seat at a quiet table in a shitty chain restaurant. I ordered, but I left the food alone; I wanted the spot more than the meal. I needed time to think. Saul was not anything close to the feeble-minded old man that David portrayed him to be — in reality, he was as sharp as a razor. And when Saul found out that David had plans to rob him, he showed that he was as deadly as a razor, too. Saul had killed David and Alvin; I was sure of that. What I didn't understand was why we were still alive. Saul wasn't shy about killing, but for some reason he delegated the chore of dealing with us to the cops and hid behind his facade of respectability. Most crooks knew only one tune, and they liked to play it over and over again. The lucky ones found a way to turn that melody into a soundtrack that lasted their whole lives. Saul knew more than a few tunes — that made him more than a regular crook. He was smarter than the average bear, and that made him more dangerous, too. He might have made jewellery, but he was no jeweller; Saul was a player. He had played all of us and won.

I got up from the table and paid for what I should have eaten. I left the restaurant and headed towards the airline counter. It wasn't time for a rematch — it was time to leave town.

CHAPTER FORTY-FOUR

It wasn't until a month after everything in New York had gone to shit that something pinged on a thought buried deep in my subconscious. I had gotten away clean, but clean didn't pay the bills. It didn't take me long to pick up a line on a job out of Detroit.

At the time, I was sitting in a bar watching two bank employees enjoying a quiet conversation over wine. One was the bank manager; the other was a teller who the manager's wife didn't know he was sleeping with. The couple made a habit of leaving the bank within minutes of one another for a quiet lunch break together. I had tailed the couple to the bar and chose a stool on the other side of the room that allowed me to watch their interaction in the reflection of the mirror behind the bar. The manager always left work as fast as possible to maximize his adultery time, but I wasn't interested in whatever action he could grab on his break. Rushing bred mistakes, and I was looking for any missteps I could take advantage of.

"Buy me a drink?"

The slurred words had pulled my eyes away from the mirror and my quiet surveillance. The fifty-something beside me had done it all the hard way. Deep lines on her face mapped out a lifetime measured in bottles and packs. Everything about her was thin; her hair, her body, her eyebrows. She had plucked her face clean long ago and in memoriam, she sketched two thin dark lines that plunged sharply after they passed her pupils. The result was a set of eyebrows that resembled the claws of monsters drawn by children.

"I'm Joyce."

Joyce didn't need a response to keep talking. I guessed this conversation was a script she recited often.

"I've seen you in here before."

That got my attention.

When she saw that my eyes were on her, she smiled and leaned in closer. "Have you noticed me?"

"Yes."

"You felt it, too, didn't you? We have some kind of connection."

"No."

She reversed course on her lean. "That was rude."

"No. It was the truth," I said.

She put a hand on her hip. "The truth can be rude."

"No," I said, "it can't. The truth is what it is. Any weight given to it is on the part of the subject."

"What?"

I checked the mirror and saw the bank teller looking at the two of us out of the corner of her eye.

"Sit down. Let me buy you a drink."

Joyce smiled and I forced myself to do the same. "That's more like it," she said.

I signalled the bartender and checked the mirror. The teller had stopped looking.

"You're not off the hook, y'know."

I looked at Joyce.

"For being rude."

I sighed. "I have been in this bar exactly two other times in the middle of the day. That was enough for you to notice me and size me up as a mark."

"That your name?"

I looked at Joyce again. She wasn't smiling now, but there was a smug grin. I liked the grin.

"I think you come here every day and play the same game. You come on to a guy, and if he turns you down, you play the victim until he smoothes things over by buying you a drink."

The bartender put a glass in front of Joyce on his way past us. He didn't need to ask her what she wanted. She took a small sip of what looked like straight rye.

"How often do you get the date?"

She looked me in the eye. "I do alright."

"How often do you get the drink?"

Joyce pulled her eyes away from mine and took another sip; this one larger. "More than I get the date." Joyce looked at me over the rim of her glass. "You think you got me all figured out, don't you?"

"I do. You got your drink, so stop pretending I offended you."

"You don't know the first thing about me, mark."

I grunted a response and nursed my drink some more. If Joyce stormed off, the couple from the bank would likely notice. I didn't want their attention, so I needed Joyce to stick around a bit more.

"Tell me what I missed."

"Where do I start?" She sighed and put down her drink. "What's the point? Guys like you don't change your mind. You're no different than everyone else. You see me in here and you decide this is all I am. You never think that I'm more than this, that maybe you've just missed something — something important that would show you the real me. But it's like I said —"

I wasn't listening anymore; I wasn't watching the couple anymore, either. I was thinking about what Joyce had just said. I stood and put a twenty on the bar. "Get yourself another — on me." I walked out of the bar and away from the bankers.

I walked straight to my car and drove back to the motel I had been living out of that week. I powered up my laptop and downloaded David's slideshow off the website I had backed it up to. I had watched the slideshow countless times looking for information that would help me get inside. This time, I watched it not for angles on how to get inside but for information on the man who had wanted to get us there. I had spent a lot of time thinking about how Saul had conned the three of us and not enough time thinking about how David had conned us. I had missed something — something important that would have shown me the real him.

I found it on slide twenty-seven. It was an image of an office. David had told us that the offices were locked when they weren't in use, so he took pictures of the only one he could access without raising suspicion — his own. David's office had a desk, a computer, some kind of jewellery microscope, and various other tools that were presumably for working on jewellery. The equipment made sense. What didn't make sense was the money counter in the middle of his workspace. The jewellery equipment was arranged around it. Arranged was the key word. The machine was in the centre of the desk. What kind of jeweller had a bill counter on his desk? Answer: the kind who counts money more than he counts stones. David wasn't wholly a jeweller, either.

I thought back to David's pitch. David had been with Saul for years; he was his number two. David ran the business and waited for Saul to let him ascend to the throne. Saul was like a father to David — words the old man echoed. I didn't take that to be a coincidence; the best cons always had elements of the truth sewed into them, and I had just found one of the seams. Another seam was David's motivation. He was willing to be our inside man and put himself at risk because he was tired of waiting for Saul to turn over the business. He wanted it all for himself, and he thought the robbery would make that happen. Why would a man turn against someone who had been a second father to him? I thought about it, but it didn't really require a lot of thought. People looking to steal were motivated by money, lust, or power; sometimes, it was a combination of the three.

This job felt like money was at the core. David was Saul's number two and yet he called a meeting at his Jersey townhouse. The ten of us barely fit in David's basement. I bet there would have been more room in any of Saul's bathrooms. However Saul felt about David, he obviously didn't love him enough to share the wealth, so David decided to take what he thought was his. But he couldn't do it himself. David hired us to do it for him. That's not the usual gangster MO. Most times, a coup is Shakespearean in body count; you can't rest easy in your new seat of power if you think the old king is coming for revenge. David's play didn't make any sense; unless the crime was about more than the money — maybe it was about insurance. Something in those safes had the power to neutralize Saul.

The only problem was David; he wasn't anywhere close to as slick as he thought he was. His boss figured out what he was up to and put him, and his brother-in-law, underground. The jeweller didn't do his own dirty work, though; Saul was a real professional, and he had people for the dirty business. He wasn't about to pull that fancy little pistol to settle his own score.

The last thought stayed with me. It was something I had heard before. Donny of Donny's Diamonds had said something similar about his fence. When we pressed him about the name of his guy, he got uncharacteristically quiet. He said his contact wouldn't shoot him with his fancy pistol; instead, he'd have some Russian do it for him. I had been so focused on getting the diamonds that I ignored what Donny had said. He was talking about Saul. Saul was Donny's fence. I cursed under my breath. Saul was ahead of me again. I had robbed Donny and then tried to pass his stones off to the same guy who was going to fence everything else in the shitty jeweller's store. We stood in the street after we showed him the stones and wondered what took an old man so long to get dressed. Saul was likely on the phone with Donny. It took him ten minutes to confirm his suspicions and get his pants on. He had time to work out what came next on the drive over to Mendelson's.

We had lost because we had never been playing the same game. Away from the board, I gained some perspective and saw where I had gone wrong.

Someone had once passed off the words of Mark Twain as their own in an effort to impress me and sound smart. The guy botched the quote, but there had been enough there for me to track down the rest. *To a man with a hammer, everything looks like a nail.* David had put a hammer in my hand and convinced me that there were nails everywhere. Standing in that motel room, I now understood that David had led me on from the start. Everything he had set in motion had been tainted with his own personal machinations. David had thought he had all of the angles covered, but he miscalculated Saul's intelligence and his capacity for violence. Saul was no old man. He had years on his body, but they were just camouflage; age hadn't touched the real man underneath. Saul had derailed everything David had orchestrated and left me holding the hammer. Despite the missteps, the realization made me smile. There were no more nails, but I wasn't ready to put down the hammer. A hammer can do a hell of lot more than hit nails — especially when you stop worrying about being quiet.

Detroit went better than New York, and when it was over, I banked the money and used the downtime to take a vacation to the Big Apple. I spent a couple of weeks watching the old man walk back and forth from his store at the same times every day. I was seeing the same things I had seen before, but I was looking at them with fresh eyes. I no longer had any illusions about who Saul was, and that changed things. Before I left the city, I made a few trips back to Mendelson's after hours. I timed my visits between laps of the security company prowl car and used the quarter of an hour to explore the building up close.

The vacation ended when I got word of a job down South; someone wanted to steal something in Miami and they needed a crew and a plan. The Miami job took longer than I had initially thought it would, but I didn't mind — it gave me plenty of time to plan what I would do when it was over. I left Florida with more than I arrived with and a contact who had more work he wanted to throw my way. I agreed to come back after I took a vacation.

"You want to take a vacation from Miami?"

Arnold Miller was an ex-professional poker player who learned the hard way that he wasn't very good at cards. Learning that you're bad at gambling is usually a lesson taught by serious people whose idea of homework is a trip to the emergency room. Arnold should have been an expert at walking on crutches, but he never needed them. In addition to being a bad poker player, Arnold was one hell of a second-storey man. Arnold paid off his loans with stolen jewellery and never saw a reason to go back to the cards. Arnold made a hundred times what he lost, and he invested in a few nightclubs. The clubs were a safer source of income and they made money, but not enough. Arnold could have easily gone back to stealing jewellery, but he was smart enough to know that he was too out of shape to start climbing through windows again. He was a thief who was too old to steal, so he did the next best thing — he financed other people's crimes. Arnold put up money for almost anyone as long as he got the first cut of the take, plus interest — a lot of interest.

I looked at the silver-haired man sitting poolside in a Hawaiian shirt. He was a man who had totally embraced Miami, and he had the skin-cancer scars to prove it. "I need to go up North," I said.

"Jesus Christ, North? Don't tell me you ski."

I shook my head. "I'm going to visit some friends."

Arnold smiled. "It's cute that you think a guy like you can have friends. People like me are all you get — remember that. And remember to call me when you're done pretending you're a regular person."

The work in Detroit and Miami had been intermissions; they made me money, but, more importantly, they bought me time — time to think and time to plan. Ten months later, I was ready to go back.

I called Tommy's Super Fantastic Funporium and asked to speak with the manager. The call was transferred and went directly to voicemail.

After a saccharine greeting and a monotone beep, I said, "My name is Irving Steele, and I was interested in booking a private room. I need space for eight plus myself." I gave some vague details about my party before leaving my number. Jake would get the voicemail and understand the real message immediately. A message from a man named I. Steele let him know what business the caller was interested in. The number of people was the amount to add, or take away, from each digit of the phone number; asking for a party of eight plus myself meant Jake would add nine to every number I gave him. The number was to a prepaid burner phone I had picked up a few hours before.

Jake called me back two hours later.

"Yeah."

"Mr. Steele?"

"My friends call me Wilson."

"Long time, pal."

"Ten months."

"You got something in mind? Or are you looking for work?"

"I need a crew."

"Tell me what you're looking for? I'll reach out to the right people."

"How about I give you names instead."

"We can do it that way. But you know the deal; I do the reaching out."

"I understand," I said.

"Who are you looking for?"

"I need the same crew I had last time."

There was a long sigh. "You know you can't have the *same* crew. If memory serves, two of them are dead and one of them was left outside a hospital. And, if I'm being honest, I don't remember that job as anything more than a clusterfuck. When I make those calls, the boys will want to know who's reaching out, and I'll have to tell them it's you. Do you really think they'll want to sign on after everything that happened?"

"Their choice to make, Jake. Like you said, you make the calls, not *the calls*."

Jake was a middleman, not my mother. But the questions on his mind would be the same ones on everyone else's. I needed Jake on board, so I gave him some answers.

"The job never sat right with me. Alvin's brother-in-law held back. We went in with the wrong information, and it cost us. We never had a shot at pulling that job off — not like that."

"So what changed?"

"Ten months gave me time to think. Time to plan. I got a way to do it right."

"And this way requires seven other people?" Jake sounded skeptical.

In the eight months I had spent waiting for the right time to come back, I had envisioned this conversation. "We lost our inside man, but I still need inside information."

"I don't follow."

"The eight of us heard the pitch, Jake. Eight different people with eight different skill sets heard the same thing, but there is no chance they remember it the same way. The two safecrackers would have picked up on some things the driver would have missed. And the tech guy would have noticed details that the safe guys didn't pick up on. I need everyone back so that we can piece the entire puzzle together. For what I have in mind, I need the original crew. Tell them there's five in it just for showing."

Jake mulled it over. He finally said, "I'll make some calls, but I can't make any promises."

"Whoever believes promises, Jake?"

CHAPTER FORTY-FIVE

Everyone showed up. Like the last meeting, I had been the one to arrive first, but this time I didn't wait in the car. I had chosen a condemned building that had been boarded up and temporarily rezoned as a crack den in Hunts Point in the Bronx. The cold winter that had moved in on New York made the empty building too cold for even drug addicts to squat in, but it made it perfect for me. The apartment I picked was on the third floor; it was small, but the eight people who braved the storm were able to stand inside the living room without touching shoulders. There was only one piece of furniture — a chair I had placed opposite to the door, and no one was sitting in it. I'd also put a cooler in the centre of the room and filled it with ice and beer. Most of it was gone; Johnny and Tony had shown after the Diegos and Elliot, and they positioned themselves close to the cooler. Every beer they put down loosened their tongues, and by the time the cooler was half empty, the two men were offering unsolicited advice to whoever looked their way. If the lack of returned conversation bothered them, it didn't show.

When Miles came through the door, Johnny let out a belch that sounded like a growl. Miles walked to the cooler and took a beer. His smooth gait showed no signs of the pounding his body had taken in the getaway. He didn't take his eyes off the two men who had managed to secure a whole wall to themselves.

"Can we just get this thing started?" Tony asked from somewhere under his moustache.

"And where are the five Gs we're owed for making it to this meeting? Should be more if you ask me. The weather made it a bitch to get here," Johnny said.

"We're one short," I said. "Give it a minute."

"Fuck," Johnny said. "He mean the girl? You telling me we're still letting her in on this?"

"Yup," I said.

Johnny laughed. "Whoever heard of a woman driving getaway?"

No one answered. I imagine any one of us had, but we all recognized that talking to Johnny was a waste of time.

"Was that rhetorical? Because I imagine plenty of women drove getaway after they met you."

The Diegos looked over to the doorway and laughed when they saw Monica standing in it. "Nice to see you again, chica."

"You too," Monica said.

"There's beer in the cooler," I said. "The chair is for you."

"You gonna pull it out for her?" Tony said, laughing and clapping his partner on the back.

Johnny leered at Monica. "Just so you know, if he won't pull it out, I will."

The two men laughed at their own jokes and emptied what was left in their bottles.

Monica looked at the two much bigger men. "I'll stand."

I stepped into the middle of the room. "I want to thank everyone for making the trip. I know things didn't go as planned last time —"

"You can say that again." If Diego #2 was trying to make a joke, no one could tell by his face.

"We're hoping to change that," I said.

Diego #1 took a step forward. "What's changed?"

"I have a way inside," I said.

Everyone was quiet while they took in what I had said. Elliot, in rumpled clothes that looked like they'd been worn since the last meeting, cleared his throat and spoke first. "How?"

"In a minute."

"Because you're going to pay us the money you promised us first right?" Johnny said.

"Soon," I said. "When David and Alvin died, we called off the job. Some of us stayed on."

If the news surprised any of the men in the room, I didn't see it on their faces. I looked every person in the eye, saving Miles for last. He had been watching the faces in the room, too. I moved my eyes over Miles's eyes and looked at his hands.

I continued, "I saw a way to move on the diamonds. The plan was less flashy than what David had planned and required less bodies."

"And?" Diego #1 said. He was no longer leaning against

the wall with his arms crossed. He was interested in what I had to say.

"It didn't go as planned."

"So now you want us to help you try again? Who the hell is going to sign on with someone who fucked things up the first time?"

I looked at Johnny. "Hear me out."

"Fuck that," he said. "I showed up. That was the deal. Give me my money, so I can walk out of here."

"Hear me out."

Johnny heard something in my voice that the primal part of his brain understood. He stayed on the wall.

"The job had unforeseen complications," I said.

Diego #1 was still interested. "What kind of complications?"

"Someone ratted us out to the cops."

Johnny snorted.

"It was meant to take us off the board."

"It was a pussy move," Johnny said with a sneer.

"No argument here, partner," Tony said.

"There was something else," I said.

I watched the faces in the room. Johnny and Tony waited for the next revelation with the patience of men who have stared at bars for years. The Diegos were equally blank. If any of the men knew what I was talking about, they weren't letting it show.

I glanced over at Elliot. He wasn't looking at me. He was looking at Tony. I followed his gaze and saw Tony catch on to the chain of looks. He gave Elliot the briefest of glances, but it was long enough for me to see it on his face. Miles saw it, too. I looked at his hands and saw two fingers showing. We had worked out a number for everyone who had showed up. Tony was the second half of the pair at the top of our list. He was a natural fit for number two. We had both seen Tony's poker face crack; Johnny had missed it.

"So this is a fucking witch hunt," Johnny said. "You went solo, got burned, and now you're looking for someone to pin it on. Well, maybe you should look in the mirror. Some fucking planner you turned out to be." The burly con took a step towards the centre of the room. "Pay me what you promised, so I can get the fuck out of here."

"Wasn't the deal," I said.

"The fuck it wasn't."

"The deal was you show up and hear my proposition and then you get the money."

"Great," Johnny said. "It's a fucking timeshare presentation."

I ignored the con and walked to the cooler. "Hear what I have to say and then decide whether or not you want to walk."

I tapped the cooler. "You want another?"

"I want my money," Johnny said.

"Me too," echoed Tony.

"Then I'll finish what I have to say." I reached for the cooler, but I didn't reach for the lid; instead, I took hold of the handle and brought the whole end of the cooler off the floor. A tidal wave of ice, water, and beer bottles splashed across the floorboards.

Diego #1 backed to the wall. "What the hell?"

The hell was a Mossberg pump-action shotgun with a pistol grip. The cooler was the biggest one Walmart carried and it easily had enough space for three bags of ice and a case of beer; the base was also large enough to conceal the hole I had cut into the floor. Everyone's eyes were on me, but I was done talking; I wanted answers. I racked the slide and sent an unspent shell to the floor. The demonstration was careless, but shotguns have a way of persuading people to speak up. The gun only knew two words, and sometimes, the quieter sound of a shell being racked was the scarier one.

I kept the gun aimed down the centre of the room just in case anyone else wanted to add another gun to the mix. It was a mistake to go to a meeting heavy. We aren't gangsters; we're professionals, and guns are tools of the trade. Before a job, a gun is only a potential risk for drawing unwanted attention; a professional knew that, but I wagered a few people in the room decided to roll the dice and take their chances.

"Miles," I said.

Miles stepped to the hole in the floor and pulled a pistol. He backed up towards me and took up a position outside of my line of fire. With another gun covering the men in the room, I brought the shotgun up towards Elliot's ample torso.

Elliot backed away from the gun, but he only managed a step before the wall let him know there was no place else to go.

"Talk," I said.

"I don't know — What do you — I — I —"

I stepped towards Elliot and took my left hand off the shotgun. The pistol grip let me keep the gun pointed at him while I took a fistful of his shirt.

"What are you —"

I jammed the shotgun into hacker's soft neck and ended his question. I spun the much bigger man and used my grip and the gun to force him into the centre of the room and onto his knees. With two hands on the gun again, I used the end of the barrel to force Elliot's head into the hole in the floor. I could feel Elliot fighting against the gun, but I had strength and leverage on my side.

"Last chance," I said.

From the hole I heard, "We —"

Just like that, *I* became *we* and Elliot started talking.

CHAPTER FORTY-SIX

"This is bullshit," Johnny said. His broad face was florid and his voice was loud. The colour and noise were all distractions. The big man's hands were telling the real story. His heavy fists were balled tight into knuckled cannonballs. With each breath, his fists tightened and forced swelling veins to the surface of his skin. He was displaying anger and outrage, but it was all an act. The fists were the truth, and they weren't playing or acting.

"Which part?"

Johnny's brow furrowed, creating deep creases on his forehead. "Which part? All of it."

"So Elliot's lying?"

"Goddamn right he's lying."

"Why would he do that?"

"Maybe," Tony offered, "it has something to do with the gun to his head."

The taller of the two men was still next to his partner, but he was not standing where he had been a minute before.

Tony was slowly putting distance between himself and Johnny and creating two targets for me to deal with.

"Tony," I said. "Stop moving."

Tony stopped and grinned a little hand-in-the-cookie-jar sort of smile at me.

"Elliot," I said without taking my eyes, or my gun, off the two men. "You admitted to playing a part in what happened to Monica. That's bad — how bad is going to depend on how big that role was. The boys here say it was a solo performance."

"They're lying."

"Prove it," I said.

Elliot had scrambled away from the hole the second I took the gun away from his head. He had found his old spot on the wall and pressed his back into it. It was a lonely place. Everyone had backed away in fear of being collateral damage should I decide to shoot Elliot with the shotgun.

When Elliot saw that no one was going to stand up for him, he started talking. "We were after the diamonds. Same as you were. We saw the girl —"

"Monica," Miles said.

"Monica," Elliot said. "We saw her when we were following the old man. We knew she wasn't in it alone — she couldn't have been — but we disagreed on how to find her partners. I wanted to put a GPS on the car, but Johnny said there were better ways to get answers. They grabbed her, put a bag over her head, and took her back to a place we had. Johnny started working her over, but it was getting us nowhere. He kept hitting her too hard. I told them we should have used a GPS, but Tony laughed at me. He said there were better ways to track an animal to its den. That's when Tony stabbed her like this."

Elliot lunged forward with an invisible knife in his hand and stabbed the air at waist level. It didn't seem like a threatening gesture when he did it.

In preparation for the meet, I had sat down with Monica about the night she was taken. I mined her account for any information buried under the surface and came up with little more than a brief recount of events that focused heavily on the time before the abduction. Monica's memory of what had happened to her was fractured, but Elliot's story matched what little she could tell us about that night.

"And, Johnny said — He said —"

Miles spoke up from behind me. "Yeah?"

"When Tony was waving his knife around, Johnny said, *Yeah, gut that nigger*."

I looked over at the two cons. Their black eyes didn't shy away from mine. "This is bullshit. All of it."

I didn't hear the same confidence in Johnny's words.

Elliot looked at his shoes. "They knew you were getting close, so they followed her and did what they said they were going to do. I wanted to plant drugs in her car and call the cops while she was following the jeweller. Not enough drugs to get her sent away, just enough to keep her away, y'know? The cops were my idea. That wasn't enough for Johnny and Tony."

I looked at Johnny again and noticed I wasn't the only one. Out of the corner of my eye I could see Monica staring at the much bigger man. Her face was working hard to hide what she was feeling, but the tendons straining against the thin skin of her neck betrayed her.

"Fuckin' liar —"

I pointed the shotgun at Johnny and he shut up.

"They wanted Monica and whoever she was working with out of the way. They said you were greedy and that you cut us out so that you could take everything for yourselves. Tony said you cut us out, so you deserved to be cut. Those were his words. You deserved to be cut. Tony said that."

"It's just wind," Johnny said. "Words. His words. He gave you nothing but a story. If I was holding the shotgun, you'd have been the one holding the knife."

I looked over at the Diegos. They had been quiet since I introduced the shotgun. It was a smart play; talking just put you in the mix, and when the mix included a shotgun, it was best to stay out of it. Diego saw me watching him; he also saw the gun wasn't, so he figured it was safe to get involved.

He looked over at Johnny and Tony. There was no love there; there wasn't even respect. "It's a good story," he said without taking his eyes off the two men. "Real good," he looked back at me, "but a good story doesn't mean it's the truth."

I nodded. "You ever stab anyone, Diego?"

The safecracker recoiled a fraction of an inch. "What are you trying to say? Now you think I had something to do with this?"

"No," I said. "I'm asking you if you have ever stabbed anyone. I'm not talking self-defense. I mean thinking about it, and then taking a knife and doing it."

Diego #1 shook his head. "Me? No way."

"Takes a special kind of thing to want to put a piece of metal into someone else. It's why people get shot so much more than they get stabbed. Think about it. Knives are everywhere, but how often do you hear about someone getting stabbed? It happens, but nine times out of ten it's a crime of passion. People who set out to stab other people are a rare breed." I looked at Tony to make sure he was paying attention. "Rare as they are, there is one interesting thing about that type of animal. They all seem to love their knives. They have favourites, and they hold on to them even when they shouldn't."

"This going somewhere?" Diego #1 asked.

"Monica didn't see who stabbed her. I asked, but she told me that there had been a bag over her head. The bag didn't let her see faces, but it was loose enough for her to see the knife sticking out of her shirt. Seems our guy had a distinctive looking switchblade."

Monica spoke from the doorway. "A switchblade with a confederate flag on the hilt."

I looked at Tony. "Let's see your knife."

Tony smiled. "Sorry, Wilson. I don't have one."

I put the shotgun on him. "Strip."

"You serious?"

"Were you serious when you said you weren't carrying a knife?"

"You really think he'd be dumb enough to carry the same knife?" Diego #1 said.

"Only one way to find out."

"This is bullshit," Johnny said. He pointed at Elliot with

a finger that resembled a lead pipe. "This little shit. This rat —" The big man suddenly charged across the room and took hold of Elliot. Elliot was flirting with three bills, but that didn't matter to Johnny; he manhandled the fat man's bulk with ease. Johnny pivoted Elliot and drove him across the room. I barely had time to sidestep the charge; Miles managed to avoid the impending collision, but not because he was quick on his feet — it was because Johnny was quick on his. The second he was within arms' reach of Miles and his gun, Johnny shoved Elliot aside and went after the pistol. Johnny put two hands on Miles's wrist and used his substantial weight advantage to swing him around. The big man was smarter than anyone gave him credit for. He understood that the shotgun in my hands was anything but precise and that shooting at him would be the same thing as shooting at Miles. He was counting on my loyalty — I was considering it.

Behind me, Tony was moving again. His hand had already snaked around his waist and was on its way back with a nasty-looking switchblade.

"Round two, nig —" Tony got to the g at the same time Monica did. The only difference was Monica's g was for gun.

Monica had pulled a small revolver from her jacket pocket. The green army jacket could have concealed a couple of bigger guns, but she went for something low key. What wasn't low key was the sound of the gun. Two bullets shoved Tony gracelessly back against the wall and sent the knife clattering to the floor. The gunshots made my ears ring and sent the Diegos diving for cover.

Johnny ignored the shots and focused on pulling the gun from Miles's hands. Miles was putting up a fight, but Johnny's size allowed him to dominate the con man. He kneed the smaller man in the stomach and yanked the gun free only to find Monica's revolver against his neck.

"Say my name."

Johnny's eyes wrenched to the side trying to see the gun and the woman holding it.

"I want to hear you say it. Not girl, not bitch, not nigger. I want you to say my name."

Johnny swallowed and said, "Monica."

"Now say, please don't shoot me."

Johnny struggled with the words while Miles struggled to get air into his lungs again. I kept the shotgun trained on Johnny. He had two hands in the air, but Miles's gun was still in one of them. With all three guns occupied, no one was in a position to stop Elliot. He pushed himself off the wall, ran five steps, and threw himself through the window.

CHAPTER FORTY-SEVEN

"What the fuck was that?" Miles said. He straightened and grunted in pain. "Did you see that? He dove out the goddamn window."

Miles went to the hole in the glass and looked down. "There's a dumpster down there. Did anyone know there was a dumpster down there?"

I did.

"Do you see him?"

Miles leaned out. "No. Wait, yeah. He's crawling out."

Everyone, even Johnny, was engrossed in the play-by-play.

"He's limping and holding his arm, but he's walking."

"We need to go," I said. "Someone will have heard the shots." I looked at the Diegos. "Your money is in the space in the floor. Inside the envelope is an address. Meet us there at four a.m. if you want back in."

Diego #1 went straight for the hole and pulled out a stack of envelopes secured with a rubber band. He slid two out and dropped the others back in the hole. "You serious?"

I nodded.

"I thought this was about revenge."

I shook my head. "It's about the job. We have a way in, but we could never have made it work if there was someone out there waiting to double-cross us. We needed to clean house before we could move forward."

Diego #1 looked at Johnny. "That's all this was? Cleaning house?"

I looked at Tony's dead body. "That's all it was."

Diego #1 looked at Johnny and the gun against his neck. "Is the house clean yet? Can you move forward?"

Monica lifted her shirt with her free hand; she kept her other hand still. "No," she said. "I can't."

The Diegos looked at Monica's torso and the bag attached to her hip for a long time. Then, Diego #1 said, "We'll see you at four."

Everyone watched the two men leave.

Johnny called after them, but the Diegos didn't look back. They had already seen enough.

I took the gun from Johnny's hand; he didn't try to fight me. "How much of Elliot's story was on the level?"

Johnny lowered his arm and looked at his partner. "He was right about Tony, but the whole thing was Elliot's idea. He came looking for us after the meeting. He said we could do the job ourselves and make a hell of a lot more money. We were following the jeweller and saw the n —" Johnny caught himself and glanced around the room at the guns pointed in his direction, "Monica tailing him. Elliot knew it had to be you two who were with her. He didn't want to risk you making a move on the store before us, so he came to us with a way to make sure you were out of the picture."

"What was his plan for the robbery?"

"He had a way around the alarms, but that all went to shit after you tried to knock over the jeweller. The Jew upped his security, and we had to call it off."

"So stabbing Monica was just the cost of doing business?" Miles said.

On the wrong side of a room full of guns, Johnny had lost his fire. For the first time since I had met him, his voice was quiet and without a trace of bravado. "You were the ones who cut us out. It wasn't personal."

Monica jammed the gun harder into Johnny's neck. His fleshy throat enveloped most of the barrel. "I shit into a bag on my hip. Did you know that? And I'll do that for the rest of my life." She stepped back and lifted her shirt. "Look at it. Look! Look at it and tell me again how it wasn't personal."

"It — It —"

Monica stepped in close to Johnny again and pushed the gun against his head. "Can you smell it? This is the closest I've been to another man since they put it on. I live in fear of someone smelling it. All I can think about is their face. What is their face going to look like when they smell what's inside of me? But I'm not scared of you smelling it. I want you to smell it. Do you know why?"

Johnny didn't say anything. His jaw clenched in an effort to hide what the film of tears on his eyes already gave away.

Monica grabbed a fistful of Johnny's hair and forced him to look her in the eyes. "It's because I want you to die with the smell of shit in your nose."

Monica held his eyes for a long time; long enough for the smell to find its way into Johnny's nostrils. The scent sent a tremor through the big man's jaw. He broke into sobs and began to plead. Monica's own jaw remained set while she listened to every word he said. She held his gaze until he ran out of words. Then she pulled the trigger.

CHAPTER FORTY-EIGHT

I took Tony by the arm and painted a red streak across the floor with his body. His slim torso slipped inside the hole I had concealed with the cooler with little manipulation. His feet hit the subfloor, and I used the butt of the shotgun to shove the body to the side.

With Tony out of the way, I walked over to the bigger body on the floor. I took a limp arm and began to slowly drag the corpse to its above-ground shallow grave. Miles moved to take the other arm, but Monica stopped him.

"I want to do it."

Miles looked at the body; I could see him doing a mental calculation of the amount of weight she would have to pull. "Are you sure?"

"Yes."

With another pair of hands helping, I was able to get Johnny's body to the lip of the hole. I had pulled the floor up with the big ex-con in mind. Now, on the edge of the hole, I wasn't sure I had pulled enough.

I wasn't the only one thinking the hole might be a

problem. "We should try legs first," Monica said.

I nodded at Monica, and together we spun the body around. The legs fell in easily, but it became really clear really fast that Johnny's midsection was going to be an issue.

"Maybe if we angle him," Monica said.

I pulled hard on Johnny's arm and tilted the body on a forty-five degree angle. We shoved the body forward and felt the momentum come to a halt when his gut plugged the space.

"Looks like we're going to need a bigger hole."

"Shut up, Miles," I said.

"You shut up. That was a dead-on Roy Scheider."

We both looked at him.

"From *Jaws*." His eyes widened and his jaw went slack as he mimicked the old cop seeing the great white for the first time. "We're going to need a bigger boat."

We both said, "Shut up, Miles."

He didn't. "Maybe we should stand on him."

Monica ran a hand through her hair. "Stand? No, not stand." She lifted a foot and brought it down hard on the body. The next stomp had more force behind it. I stepped back. Miles and I watched silently as Johnny was forced inch by inch into the hole. With each kick, Monica lost a bit more of her composure. She began to cry, and then yell. Her screams became a roar as the body disappeared.

I went to the window and felt the cold air on my face. There weren't any sirens. I had picked the right place and time to deal with the people who had tried to deal with us. The location and date were all by design and it had almost been enough. Elliot had been smarter and more cunning than I had given him credit for. The crowded first meeting had given him camouflage. The other big personalities drew attention their way, leaving the true danger the fat computer whiz posed unnoticed.

I used the toe of my boot to kick the unopened beer bottles into the hole. I went to the next room and came back with a piece of plywood and a rug. I covered the hole with the board and rolled the rug out to hide the quick repair. I stepped back and evaluated my work. The carpet was big enough to cover the hole and bloodstains and shabby enough to blend in with the shitty room.

"Thank you," Monica said. She nodded her head towards the carpet and what was barely hiding underneath. "For that. I've been bad since it happened. Real bad. This was something I had to — something I needed to do." She took a deep breath in and slowly let it out through her nose. "I had to do this."

Miles reached out and gently put a hand on her shoulder. Monica pulled away before Miles could finish asking, "You okay?"

She nodded. "I'm better than I was this morning, but that other one is still out there. I need to find him."

I checked my watch. "That'll have to wait. We're on a timetable and we need to move."

Monica looked me in the eye. "Fine."

On the stairs, Miles asked, "Do you think they'll show?"

"Would you?" Monica asked.

He didn't even think about it. "Nope."

"Why?"

Miles looked at me. "Why? Because we killed two

members of the original crew. One right in front of them. Do you think they could ever trust us? If I were in their shoes, I'd take the five and walk."

"If we were going to kill the Diegos, if that was our plan, when would have been the smart time to do it?"

"Upstairs," Monica said.

"Exactly," I said. "They're smart enough to know that. They're also smart enough to know that Johnny and Tony had it coming. They'll show."

"Care to put money on it?" Miles asked.

I opened the stairwell door and checked the street. I motioned for Miles and Monica to follow me outside.

"That's exactly what I'm doing," I said.

CHAPTER FORTY-NINE

It took an hour to get to the truck stop and back. The snow had been falling steady for hours, and the storm of the century, the fifteenth this century, had finished warming up. The news had been speculating about the severity of the storm for days. By the day of the storm, the massive accumulations were such a foregone conclusion that the evening news gave the weatherman a break from his spot in front of the green screen in favour of an on-location report. The network set up the meteorologist in a hardware store so he could divulge weather gossip while talking to customers hurriedly buying the last of the shovels. The salt, sand, and plow trucks were out in full force, but they were all playing catch-up with the heavy snowfall.

Monica drove the plow across the highway without showing any signs that the roads were anything less than perfect. She passed cars moving at barely a crawl while avoiding the aftermath of car wrecks caused by drivers who were unprepared for the weather.

In the heavy stolen plow, the return trip to the city took half the time of the initial run to the truck stop.

"We're early," Miles said.

I nodded. "Ten minutes."

"You're welcome," Monica said.

Miles smiled and turned his head so that he could speak into Monica's ear. She shifted in her seat and put a few more inches between them.

I spoke before the con man. "Timing is everything on something like this. Ten minutes could end up being ten years."

Miles pulled away from the driver's ear and Monica eased off the gas and away from the door. "I checked the maps. I know a detour that should add a few minutes."

Monica had driven up to Buffalo a week ago and stolen the snowplow. She drove it to an abandoned barn I had found way outside the city. The barn had been our operations base for three weeks. I had come back to the city with a plan, but the plan came with a large shopping list. Monica had been instrumental in acquiring many of the items we needed; for her, the job was about more than money. The jewellery store job had cost her a piece of herself. She now carried a bag on her hip and dry swallowed pills all day long. She wouldn't say it, but I knew why she signed on with us again. She needed it to mean something. The price she had paid couldn't have been for nothing. More than that, Monica needed to know that the job hadn't been the end of her.

At three in the morning, the street was quiet. The snow-plow idled in the street, drawing attention to itself with its out-of-shape engine. Luckily, there was no one around to hear the noise coming from under the hood. The heat was turned all the way to the right, and the uncomfortably hot air coming through the vents stunk heavily of the exhaust drifting around the truck.

I shut off the heat when the stench and the temperature started to make me feel nauseous. No one complained.

"He's late," Miles said.

"The snow is slowing him down," I said.

Monica checked up and down the street. "Should we go look for him?"

"No," I said. "He'll be here soon."

"The streets are pretty terrible. Maybe he took the night off."

"Look at the road," I said. "Someone has been driving laps in the same tracks. This time of night, in this weather — it's our guy."

Five minutes later, a car with the word Cyturity painted across the doors turned off of Ninth Avenue and began a slow crawl down West 47th. Monica didn't wait for me to signal her. She pulled down her ski mask, dropped the blade, and put the plow in gear. There was a metallic scrape as the truck was forced into gear, and then the blade began to grind against the pavement as the plow picked up speed. The security car was driving in its tracks at a slow crawl. The company must have been expensive because they sprung for a current model Nissan and heavy-duty snow tires. The driver knew better than to rush in the bad weather, and the good tires ensured that the car didn't slide. All of that changed when Monica turned the wheel and hooked the plow into the side of the much smaller car. Monica had used the road to her advantage; she turned the plow at just the right time to capitalize on the skid she slid into. The plow slid a tight forty-five degree turn, and then the spinning wheels found the pavement and jolted the plow forward in its new direction. The blade connected with the side of the Nissan and drove it into the curb. The second the snowplow connected, I pulled down my own mask and opened the door. I held on to the side of the seat and waited for the impact that signalled the Nissan had been pushed as far as it could go. On the street, I circled around the back of the plow and walked straight towards the Nissan with a hammer in my hand. Monica caught sight of me in her mirrors and backed up a few feet when I was out from behind the truck. The car had been lifted onto the plow blade and only the far wheels were touching the pavement. I didn't wait for the car to get all the way to the ground before I swung the hammer into the driver's side window.

The sound of the breaking glass was overshadowed by the noise of the plow backing up. The security guard was going for his radio but my finger found the trigger first. The stun gun sent two tendrils through the hole in the window and into the chest and neck of the man behind the wheel. The guard went rigid as the electrical current overrode the commands of his brain. The stun gun crackled while I used my free hand to open the door. I eased up on the trigger and waited to see if it had been enough. The guard flopped forward and bounced off the steering wheel — it had been enough. I opened the door and secured the keys before dragging the guard out. I bound the guard's wrists and feet with zip ties that I got at the same tiny hardware store where I'd bought the hammer. The guard was still dazed when I dragged him to the rear of the car and forced him up and into the trunk. I wrapped my hand around the head of the hammer and used my loaded fist to put the driver all the way out. I closed the trunk lid and crossed the street to the idling plow. Monica was already at the rear of the big truck; I caught up with her just in time to see the tailgate fall. The sound of the metal hitting the pavement was offensively loud in the quiet stillness of the snowy morning, but it was a fitting opening for the cacophony created by the ramp that was dragged out and fitted into place. Monica had been working on the plow for a while to get it ready for what we needed it to do.

Monica climbed the custom ramp ahead of Miles and myself. On foot, she was the exact opposite of what existed when she was behind the wheel. She moved slowly and without grace, but she got there. Miles and I began to loosen straps while Monica got behind the wheel. The last strap fell away just as she turned the key. The bed had been designed to hold tons of salt; the small forklift fit just fine. I hustled down the ramp behind Miles and just a second ahead of Monica.

The second all four wheels touched the pavement, Miles and I lifted the ramp away from the tailgate and carried it to the stairs. The ramp covered the length of the stairs as though it had been made for the job — which it had. The forklift backed up the conveniently plowed street while Miles and I pulled a smaller ramp from the snowplow and placed it over the curb. It wasn't luck that the curb was empty; on the way to the meet, I had left a no-parking sign on the sidewalk. If anyone official took an interest in the sign, it wouldn't take long to realize that it wasn't kosher, but I was betting any unfortunate soul who found themselves on the street in a snowstorm wouldn't be looking too closely.

With the second ramp down, I backed up and signalled Monica. There was a hydraulic hiss as the forks lifted to a height of four feet. The engine revved and the wheels spun on the pavement before they found purchase. The forklift that we had stolen from a warehouse in Tonawanda accelerated quickly, and I wondered if Monica had spent some time under the hood. The forklift bucked when it hit the first ramp, but it stayed on course as Monica drove the machine up the second ramp and into the lacquered black door of Mendelson's Jewellery.

The forklift burst through the door and accelerated through the waiting room and into the door leading to the showroom. Miles and I entered seconds behind the forklift to see that it had gotten enough momentum to take the second door on the first try. In the small waiting room, the alarm was deafening. As we entered the showroom, the wail of the security system had some competition from the forklift that was busy smashing into display cases on its way to the final door. Monica approached the last door with more caution. If she went at it full bore, she risked hitting the rear wall; that one was all brick. Monica put the forks to the door and then slowly stepped on the accelerator; the tires didn't slide on the expensive hardwood. The door broke away from the frame and Monica proceeded forward, creating a forklift-shaped hole in the wall. By the time we caught up to the machine, Monica had lowered the forks and was in the process of narrowing their span. When she felt she had it right, I guided the metal prongs under the first safe. Monica hoisted the heavy metal box and spun it in a tight one-eighty and headed back the way it came. Miles ran ahead of the forklift and guided Monica as she lifted the safe and placed it into the bed of the snowplow.

I looked up and down the street and was happy with what I saw. The alarm had been going strong for a minute and a half, but the only sign that anyone had taken notice came from a few lights in windows that had previously been dark. I didn't worry about lights in windows; I only cared about red and blue lights on the street.

Monica whirled the forklift around and kept her foot on the break. I checked the street one more time and then spun my finger in a tight rotation — one more time.

This time, Monica went in alone. I stood on the steps and watched for any sign of a response to the alarm, but the only witness to the crime in progress was the snow. I walked down the ramp ahead of the returning forklift and let Monica handle getting the second safe into the bed. I was back with a gas can just in time to see Monica force the second safe against the first. There was a horrible screech as the heavy metal boxes scraped against the plow's bed. When the safes were in the plow, Monica turned and barrelled up the ramp again while I lifted the tailgate. I jogged up the ramp with the gas can and passed Monica on her way down. I splashed the floor of Mendelson's and the forklift and left the rest of the gas can open on the seat. I lit the fuel and waited just long enough to make sure the fire was moving in the right direction. When the flames began to climb into the driver's seat, I ran for the plow.

CHAPTER FIFTY

"**D**oesn't this thing go any faster?"

"No."

Miles looked across the seat at the side mirror. "This is a terrible getaway car."

"This ain't even a car."

"So you agree with me."

Monica checked her mirrors. "We've been over this. The only thing that isn't suspicious in this weather is a snowplow."

"We won't be on the road long," I said.

The secondary location had been a tall order. After any job, you need to go somewhere where you can lay low with whatever has been stolen. Most times it's money; this time, it was two safes stowed in the back of a snowplow, which made things considerably harder. Compounding the problem was the location. Manhattan in a snowstorm isn't teeming with places to hide a hot snowplow. It had taken a month, but I had managed to find a location close to the river. The garage had been on the market for a few months.

Judging by the state of the inside of the garage, I guessed the reason it hadn't sold was due to the half-finished renovations. I broke in a few weeks back, making sure to be loud and sloppy. I was inside for less than five minutes and then spent four hours waiting for someone to respond — no one ever did. The security stickers I saw on display had been just window dressing. The next day, I swapped all of the locks for my own. I waited a week and then checked back. No one else had been inside. I had been to the garage before the meeting, and, as usual, nothing had changed. I changed that.

Miles looked at me. "What if they don't show?"

"This again?"

Miles turned his head. "It's a valid question, Monica. If the Diegos say adios, we're left with a plow and two safes we can't open."

"They'll be there," I said.

"And if they're not?"

"They will," I said.

"How can you be sure?"

I checked my watch. "I can't be sure, but in a few minutes, we'll know."

CHAPTER FIFTY-ONE

The garage was exactly how I had left it except for the snowplow in the centre of the floor dripping water onto the concrete.

Miles was in the bed of the truck, giving the safes a closer look. "Do we have everything we need?"

I nodded. "I've been talking to some people — the right kind of people — gave me a shopping list with similar tools. I picked up what they'll need. Plus, when I had Jake reach out to them about the meeting, I made sure he relayed word that they should bring their gear."

"If they come," Miles said.

I ignored him. I wasn't having the conversation again. Miles didn't seem to have the heart for it, either. There was nothing left to do but wait, and it was easier to do that in silence.

My phone rang at four o'clock.

"That's them," Miles said. "Unless you got a girlfriend we don't know about."

I picked up. "You got my message."

"Uh hunh."

"I'm glad you decided to come in with us."

Diego #1's voice was flat. "That makes one of us."

"One? Did your brother walk away?"

"No, he came. So did Elliot."

I heard a rustle as the phone was roughly passed to someone else.

"For a good time call Diego," Elliot said. There was more gravel in his voice than before and I could hear him wheeze when he paused to take a breath. "Clever. You never stop being clever, do you? It's so goddamn annoying."

I had given Diego directions to a stop sign. Written on the sign were those words Elliot seemed to have to work to get out and a phone number. The dive out the window had taken a toll on his body; the problem was, he seemed able to pay it.

Miles and Monica stood near me with their heads tilted towards the phone in my hand.

I pulled the phone away from my ear and put it on speaker. "Put Diego back on, Elliot."

Monica and Miles exchanged a look but kept silent.

"You're not in charge, clever boy. I'm in charge. I know what you did tonight. We had the radio on while we waited. You made the news. It seems some people recorded you on their phones from their bedroom windows. The footage is already on the internet. You're celebrities. Did you know that?"

"No," I said. "The radio in the truck was broken."

Miles already had his phone out. He was on the internet looking for a report about what we had done.

"So you have the safes, but I have your safecracker."

"Cracker?" I said.

"I'm sorry to say, Diego's brother didn't make it."

"He shot him in the fucking head," Diego #1 yelled. "He just fucking shot him."

"And I'll shoot Diego here as well. Unless —"

"Unless what?"

"Unless you cut me in. I want my share."

I looked at Monica. She was looking at my face, but I could tell she wasn't seeing me. She was lost in a hate that had invaded her alongside the knife that had violated her body.

"You want the safes? You need to bring me in. I want you to lock down your partner and that bloodthirsty bitch, and then I want you to walk over here. I know —" he grunted in pain. "I know you're somewhere close. You have to be. No point setting a meeting point across town if you need someone right away. No —" he grunted again. "You're nearby. Come alone and get in the front seat. We'll drive back to wherever you are together. Try something funny, and I'll shoot Diego —"

"No," I said.

"No?" Elliot coughed. "You don't think I'll kill him? I'll do it, and then I'll call the cops and give them a tip about a suspicious snowplow in the area. They'll check with the city and it will take them about a minute to know that it's the plow they're looking for. They'll find you, Wilson. See? I'm clever, too. Just like you. But you need me because without me, you get nothing."

I hung up the phone.

Miles and Monica stared at me.

"That wasn't your call to make," Miles said.

"It was the only call to make."

"Without Diego, we have nothing."

The phone rang again. I ignored it.

"Pick it up," Monica said.

"Do it, Wilson."

I answered. It was Elliot.

"I'll do it. I will. Tell him."

Diego #1 spoke slowly and carefully. "He's got a gun to my head. He's not bluffing."

I looked at Miles and Monica and said, "Pull the trigger."

Miles yelled no, but Elliot didn't hear him. I had already hung up the phone.

A second later, we heard the shot fired at the stop sign just up the street.

CHAPTER FIFTY-TWO

"**W**hat the hell was that?" Miles screamed. "You just let him kill Diego."

Monica went for the door. She had a gun in her hand.

"No," I said.

She whirled around to face me; the sudden movement caused her to grab her side, but it didn't take the fire out of her. "He's out there."

"And he's counting on you to go looking for him. You do that, and he knows where we are. More importantly, he knows where the safes are."

Miles got into my face and shoved me with the palms of his hands. "And what good are they now, Wilson? Without the Diegos, they might as well be paperweights. No, they can't even be those because we can't even move them without a forklift. And we can't afford a forklift because we can't get into those fucking safes."

I stepped in close to Miles and spoke softly. "You keep screaming like that and he'll find us on his own."

Monica was still close to the door.

I spoke up so that she could hear me, too. "Listen, this guy is good. Really goddamn good. He walked out of an ambush tonight and got himself within feet of the finish line. You need to get past the glasses and the gut and see Elliot for what he really is. That guy is a shark dressed like Steve Wozniak. Sharks don't share and neither does Elliot. He doesn't want his piece; he wants the whole score. He wanted me to secure you two and then meet him alone. Why?"

Monica turned from the door. "To kill you."

I nodded.

"But if he did that, he'd have no idea where we were. How would that help him?"

I shook my head. "You're thinking like a person. Think like a shark. If I showed up, it would confirm that he was right and that we were close. As soon as I was dead, he'd use the snow against us and follow my tracks straight back to you."

Miles nodded to himself. "He was right. He is as clever as you are."

Monica looked at me; then at Miles. "What am I missing?"

Miles took a step towards Monica. "He was never going to let Diego live."

"Why not?"

"He knew Wilson wouldn't walk out to him, and he knew we'd never agree to letting him tie us up. He knew all of this, but he still put it out there."

"Why?"

"So Wilson would say no," Miles said. "Then he called back so that we could hear him shoot Diego. We'd blame

Wilson. It was an impossible situation, but we'd blame him all the same. That would be enough."

"For what?"

"To drive a wedge between us. Maybe thin our numbers if he's lucky." Miles stepped closer to Monica. "He saw you back there. He saw that look in your eye. The one you have right now. He knows that you want nothing more than to kill him. He's counting on that."

Monica's chin dropped to her chest. "He's using me again. Goddamnit, he's using me again!"

"And now you've figured him out, and you want to go out that door even more," I said.

Miles took another step closer to Monica. "Like I said, Elliot is clever. He was sure killing Diego would drive a wedge between us. He saw us talking. He knows there is something between us."

Monica laughed without any humour. "One time almost a year ago doesn't put something between us."

It was Miles's turn to laugh. "That's where you're wrong. One time leaves a trace that a clever guy like Elliot can spot. He was betting that I would blame Wilson for letting Diego die and I'd side with you. It was a smart play. After all, Wilson let one of our crew die. Who could stand with a man after he did something like that?"

"So why are you?"

Miles smiled. "Because I know something Elliot doesn't know."

"What's that?"

Miles looked at me. "I already knew exactly what kind of bastard Wilson is."

"So what's he doing now?" Monica said.

"He's not calling the cops," Miles said.

"You don't think so?"

"He's looking for us," I said.

"Good luck. Those tire tracks are long gone."

"He won't need them," I said. "He knows he's close. There are only so many places around here to hide a truck and provide the necessary space to open two safes without raising any alarms. With enough time, he'll find us."

"So do we wait for him to show up? Or do we go after him?"

"Good question," Miles said.

"Neither," I said. "He's pushing us, and that means he has an agenda. We can't be sure if he's banking on us to stay put, or go after him."

Monica looked confused. "So we do nothing?"

"We'll move," I said, "but not when he wants, or where he wants."

CHAPTER FIFTY-THREE

Something bothered me about the death of the Diegos. It wasn't their actual dying that bothered me. They had been in this line of work long enough to know the risks. What bothered me was how willing Elliot had been to kill the two men capable of opening the safes. I looked at the huge boxes. They were designed to thwart any type of unwanted entry. To get inside without the combination, you needed the hands of a surgeon and the knowledge of an engineer. So why was Elliot so quick to knock off the two people with the right mix of fingers and lobes? The answer: he didn't need them. I smiled. He didn't need them, and I knew why.

I had been keeping tabs on Saul. He had added security since the job went south. The additional security wasn't a new system for the store; it was a personal bodyguard for himself. A goon who shopped at the big-and-tall shop now picked up Saul at his door and remained in his shadow for the entire day. The message was clear: he wasn't worried about the business; Saul was worried about Saul. His fears were easy for me to spot; now I wondered if anyone else had been watching.

Saul hadn't changed his phone number; there was no point. We knew where he worked and where he lived; an angry phone call was the least of his worries.

He picked up right away. "Yeah?"

"He called you, didn't he?"

There was a short pause. "Detective Lock. That was your name, wasn't it?"

"It was. And that wasn't an answer, Saul. He made you an offer, didn't he?"

Saul was quiet for a few seconds. I understood. There were a lot of ways things could go tonight, and he wanted to make sure all ways pointed towards him. "You don't mean the police, do you? Because they called me."

"No," I said. "Not the police. One man. Unaffiliated."

Saul laughed. "After hearing from you again, I get the sense that he had an affiliation once."

"What did he offer?"

"That is between us."

"Whatever it was, you agreed to it."

"Did I?"

"Yes," I said. "It's the only way this plays."

"I'm afraid I don't follow."

"The body count is too high for the pay to be low."

Saul laughed again. "I don't know what you're talking about, Detective, but if you're asking me to feel bad about the deaths of men who robbed me, I don't think I can do that."

"Tell me what you're paying him."

"Why would I do something like that?"

"You should play ball, Saul. After all, you're hardly the only game in town."

"What are you talking about?"

"I'm talking about something your new partner missed. David wasn't after diamonds. He told us a great story about being overlooked and underappreciated by a man who was set on going down with his sinking ship, but it was all bullshit. He didn't care about the diamonds. What he really cared about was what was inside the second safe. David told us that you were senile and that you had been buying uncut diamonds to fill orders that were all in your head. But those were all lies. You're not that guy, Saul. But David wanted into that safe all the same. I'm guessing he wasn't lying about the uncut stones. I think he was telling the truth about that, but I don't think the rocks in your safe were ever destined to be jewellery. Those stones are for a different kind of client."

"It's a good story," Saul said.

"It gets better. I think there was something else in that safe of yours. Something that could be more valuable than diamonds if the right person was holding it. If I had to guess, I'd say it was your books — the real books. I think David was after the business. He was planning on climbing over you, and inside that safe was the last rung."

"I don't know what you're talking about."

"That's fine. I told the same story to some other people, and they liked what I had to say."

"I'm guessing he doesn't mean us," Monica whispered.

Miles ignored the playful jab and just shook his head.

I was in his territory, and he wanted to see where the con was leading Saul.

"Is that right?"

"They liked it because they had heard it before from David. Apparently, he had been talking to these same thick-necked Russians about moving their money overseas using uncut diamonds. He assured them that he would have everything in place to make a seamless transition. He even offered a buy-in to show he was serious. I think that would have been what he did with his cut of the job. It was a lot of money, but he wouldn't miss it; not with the numbers he would be pulling in when he was in charge."

The whole story was bullshit. I had even plagiarized some of the words from the conversation we had had with Donny. My gut told me that his mysterious fence was Saul, but it didn't really matter if my gut was right or not. Donny had a fence who laundered Russian money with uncut diamonds. Even if it wasn't Saul, the story was plausible and plausibility was all I needed. I didn't need to convince him that what I said was the truth, I just needed to convince him that what I was saying could be the truth.

The sound of me hitting the jackpot was no sound at all. Saul was suddenly on the losing side of a game he didn't even know he was playing.

"Give me a number, Saul. How much are you willing to pay to get back what's yours?"

"You can't be serious."

"You think I'm calling you to gloat. There's no money in the egg on people's face. I don't care about getting the better of you. I care about something else."

"And what's that?"

"I care about getting paid. Tonight I had planned to empty your safes and walk away, but things went sideways on us."

Saul's laugh had barely a trace of humour in it. "I can't say I'm sorry to hear that."

"No? You should be. Had things played out the way I had intended, you'd have taken a hit on the stones, but you would have survived. As for the other things; I would have found whatever was in your personal safe and I would have left it behind."

Saul didn't believe me. "Really?"

"I'm a professional thief, Saul, not a blackmailer. The diamonds would have been enough. They still are. That's why I want a number. Otherwise, I have to go with the only other bidder. They wanted whatever David was selling, and they are just as interested in what I have. Whatever is in that safe is enough to buy me a jugger on short notice."

"Jugger?"

"A safecracker, Saul. Elliot killed mine after he talked to you, so I had to go with the backup plan. Want to guess what the Russians will do with what they find in that safe?"

Saul didn't want to.

"My bet is you would find yourself a junior partner in your own business."

"It's a little late to pretend that you care about what happens to my business."

"When I make the call to the Russians, what are my chances that they'll play fair?"

Saul laughed.

"I'm not saying it can't be done, but there will be risks. I'm confident I can manage the risks, but they're there just the same. But no matter how it plays for me, you'll lose everything."

"Unless I make you a better offer," Saul said.

"Yes."

"No."

"No?"

"No, you don't want an offer. I've been doing this for too long to think that you are waiting on me for a number. You know what you want, so just say it and stop wasting my time."

My number was small. "One safe," I said.

Saul laughed.

"You're insured, so there's no loss. After seeing how you operate, I wouldn't be surprised if you made a profit."

"In exchange for my safe?"

"You get an address where you'll find your other safe."

"Do you really expect me to trust you?"

"No."

"I suppose this is the part where you tell me I have ten seconds to decide."

"Ten seconds? No, you have until my call-waiting beeps. When that happens, I hang up on you and take my chances with the Russians."

The line went quiet. I waited. Miles lifted his hands in a silent demand for an update, but I ignored him.

After three minutes, I said, "Time's up."

Saul gave me the combination.

CHAPTER FIFTY-FOUR

Miles and Monica scrambled into the plow bed and moved to a safe. I repeated the combination out loud and Monica worked the dial. Miles lifted a thumb into the air the second the door started to open.

"Alright, I held up my end of the bargain. Where is my safe?"

I ended the call as I crossed the garage to the Toyota I had dropped off several hours before. I popped the trunk and pulled out two duffel bags. I threw the bags into the bed of the plow before climbing up to get a look at what we had stolen. The safe was six feet tall and contained twelve velvet-lined shelves. Everything that had been in the display cases had been stored in the safe.

"I can't believe that worked," Monica said as she cleared out the shelves dedicated to the rings. "I can't believe he just let us into one of his safes."

"It was a smart play," Miles said.

"How do you figure?" Monica asked as she began

grabbing necklaces. "How is handing everything over the smart play?"

"He's already lost it. You saw those people hanging out their windows with their phones in their hands. YouTube is going be his alibi. His insurance will have no choice but to pay up for everything. Wilson was right, a crafty guy like him will probably make money on losing his jewellery. Letting us into this safe is meaningless. Saul knew that all along, and he figured it was an acceptable gamble if it gave him a shot at the other safe."

"Then why did he wait so long to give it up?"

"He was waiting on Elliot," I said. "He was sitting in his house waiting, praying, for the sound of gunfire to break out. When I told him I was going to hang up the phone, he had no choice but to give up the combination." I looked at Miles. "He didn't give up the numbers because it was the smart play, he did it to keep the numbers manageable."

Miles thought about it. "He didn't want the Russians involved."

"Not with only one man out there working for him. Giving us the combination means Elliot only has three people to worry about, and it keeps us occupied and in the same spot. The game isn't over."

Miles finished loading his bag and put it on his shoulder. He offered to help Monica, but she shoved him away. "So how do we play it?"

I looked at the two duffel bags. "He's nearby, and he knows we're going to move soon. The weather gives him an advantage because any car on the road will stand out and leave a trail. Elliot will set himself up in a way that takes advantage of the conditions."

"So," Miles said.

"So we take advantage of the one thing he can't change."

"What's that?"

"He's one man —"

"And?" Monica said.

"And we have two cars."

CHAPTER FIFTY-FIVE

"**S**o we're going to make a run for it?" Monica said.

I closed the trunk of the Toyota. "We're not running. We're getting away."

I tossed the keys to the plow to Monica; she didn't try to catch them. "We're not getting away. Elliot is getting away."

"The job is over," I said. "It's time to go."

"No."

"No?"

"He is not getting away. He did it once, and I am not letting him do it again. He doesn't get to walk away, not after what he did to me."

I looked at Miles.

"Monica," he said. "We —"

She snapped her chin towards Miles. "What are you, his fucking dog? He says that it's time to go and you start jumping up and down with your tail wagging."

"It's not like that, Mon."

"Oh no? So was it both of your idea to leave me on the ground in front of the emergency room after Elliot stabbed me?" Monica turned her head and looked me in the eyes. "Or was it his?"

Miles stammered.

"You know what? Don't even bother, Miles. I know what happened, and so do you. He left me there because I was inconvenient. I was damaged goods, so he cut me loose. I spent months trying to learn how to live with shitting in a bag, and you know what, Wilson? I never did. I never learned how to live with it. The only thing that made living possible was the thought that one day I would be able to pay back every motherfucker responsible. And now you're ready to cut and run again because the job is over."

Monica lifted her shirt. The knife that had been used on her had left a long fat scar that had healed raised and pink. Her smooth dark skin could do nothing to hide the evidence of the violation. On her side was a pouch affixed to a strap that ran over her shoulder like the strap of a purse. I looked at the wound and the bag, and then I looked at Monica.

She pulled down her shirt and adjusted it four or five times. "The job isn't over — not for me; not with Elliot still out there."

I nodded and walked over to the keys that had hit the ground. I went back to the Toyota and got out the two duffel bags. "You can keep the Toyota," I said. "I'll take my chances with the plow."

Monica was caught off guard. "What?"

"I'll put some distance between us and here and then find a car to get the rest of the way to the safe house. You can meet up with us when you're ready."

"You're leaving?"

"I'm sticking to the plan," I said.

"You're leaving."

"The job is done," I said. "It's time to walk away."

"'Cause that's what you do best, right? You walk away and leave the rest of us to fend for ourselves."

I opened the driver's side door and tossed the first bag into the plow. "Miles, you staying or going."

Miles looked at Monica. She saw the answer on his face before he said a thing.

"No."

Miles looked at his shoes.

"Miles, no. No!"

"I'm sorry, Mon."

She shook her head. "No. No, no, no."

I walked to the garage door and pulled it up. The clatter of the metal sounded like robotic applause. Snow and wind forced its way into the opening and immediately began feasting on the heat.

"You're doing it to me again," Monica said. "I can't believe you're leaving me again. You — you —"

I missed the first half of the draw because Miles was standing between the two of us. When I saw Miles react, the gun was already on its way to being level with centre mass. Miles dove for the floor, but Monica wasn't aiming at him. She was aiming at me.

The bullet hit me just above the right hip and folded me over. The next blow came from the concrete floor. With both hands occupied with the new hole in my torso, my head was left to fend for itself. The concrete caught my skull with a total lack of grace.

Time and space became unreliable after that. One second, Monica was across the room; the next, she was standing over me.

"Did you ever wonder why I signed back on for this? After what happened to me, do you think I care about the money?" Monica jabbed my chest with the gun. "I came back for revenge. I thought you understood that. I thought you were different. I don't know why. After what you did to me, I don't know why I thought you were. I see now that I was wrong."

I lifted my head and strained to look at the wound. The blood that flowed out of the hole was dark in colour and seeped through my fingers with no sign of stopping.

"Monica, please, it's not too late. We can get him to a hospital."

She lifted the gun towards Miles. He backed away. "I wonder. Did you fight that hard for me?"

I took one slippery hand off my stomach and went for my gun while Monica was occupied. She saw me moving and kicked me in the stomach before I got the gun out of the holster. I howled into the floor and braced myself for another attack, but it never came. Instead of getting in a few more licks, Monica just picked up my gun and put it into one of her jacket pockets. "Hurts, doesn't it? I think it's good that you're learning that."

"Monica, you don't have to do this," Miles pleaded.

Monica pointed her gun at the con man. "Do me a favour, Miles. Shut up."

Miles looked at the gun and did as he was told.

"Thank you. Now, use two fingers to take your gun out

of the holster and slowly place it on the floor."

"What happened to you?"

"I stopped waiting around for my revenge. It's like I told you before, Miles. I do what I have to do, and I'm not waiting a second longer to get what's mine. Now give me your gun."

Miles did as he was told and then Monica shot him in the leg. The con man went down howling. Monica ignored him and kneeled next to me. Her breath on my ear was warm, and her voice as soft as mother's lullaby. "I'm going to give you a choice, and that's more than you gave me, so you should be grateful. You can take your chances here with me, or you can make a run for it."

I turned my head so I could see her eyes.

"Run away, Wilson. I won't try to stop you."

I didn't wait for the catch. I rolled onto my stomach and groaned. I placed two palms on the concrete and pushed myself up. I put a foot flat on the ground and promptly lost my balance. When I tried to reposition my hands, my palm found the pool of blood that had leaked from my body. The surface of the blood had been exposed to the cold air blowing through the open door, and a crust of ice had already formed on the top of the red puddle. My arm slid on the blood and my chest and face slammed into the concrete. I growled through the pain and crawled through the blood towards the wall. I used the chains next to the garage door to get me onto my feet.

I turned to look at Monica and saw Miles crawling towards me. His leg was painting a thick line on the floor.

"You're staying, Miles," Monica said. "Or would you prefer I use language you'll understand? Heel, doggy."

Miles looked at Monica. "Why are you doing this?"

"She's going fishing," I groaned.

"Fishing?"

"With live bait."

I stumbled out the door and took the brunt of the wind against the side of my face. I let the wind choose my direction and put the blowing snow to my back. I cleared the garage and put my shoulder to the side of the building. Monica didn't shoot me for revenge — at least not only for revenge. She shot me because she wanted me out on the street. The bullet was well placed; it was a walking wound. More importantly, it was a trailing wound. Behind me, the white snow was defaced with a sloppy red streak of plasma graffiti. Elliot was out here looking for us; Monica was counting on it. She was also counting on Elliot following the shots to me. She didn't care what Elliot did with what he found; her only concern was that Elliot saw the fat red line leading to the garage, where she'd be waiting. I guessed that she had a plan to use Miles to her advantage, too.

Gut shots are often called walking wounds because you can walk with them; no one ever said how far you'd get. Wounded, on foot in a snowstorm, with no weapon — I had little chance of survival. I definitely wouldn't make it past Elliot, but what if I could get Elliot past me. I turned and looked at the footprints in the snow. The garage was still open, and the light that spilled out made my boot prints visible. I counted over thirty. It was enough. I stopped fighting to stay on my feet. The snow caught me and held me tight while the storm began the slow process of burying my body.

CHAPTER FIFTY-SIX

I heard the car coming. I couldn't tell if it was Elliot; the snow had been falling on me for a while and the wind had helped it do its job faster. Buried in a shallow grave of snow, I had no way of telling how long I had been laying there, but I wasn't cold anymore and that meant it had been too long.

The car stopped next to me and the door opened. It was time to see if Elliot was as clever as he said he was. It's a scary thing relying on someone else to be exactly what you think they are; especially when what you think they are is a cold, calculating murderer. If Elliot was any other kind of murderer, he would get to be one again really soon. But if he was the kind of killer I thought he was, he would know that it would be a terrible idea to shoot me. A gunshot would announce his presence and put anyone inside on guard. If it was Elliot, and he was clever, he'd leave the body alone, but he'd check it.

He kicked me first. The snow did little to protect me, but the cold had made everything numb. I heard the kicker grunt and then felt rough hands pull me up by my jacket.

"Heh, looks like someone did my job for me," Elliot said before he dropped me. I heard another grunt as he straightened up. "Let's see what they left me."

I listened to Elliot's boots as they trudged through the snow. I counted the steps waiting for thirty. At twenty-five, I opened my eyes and looked to my right. The car was still there and it was still running. I risked a look towards the garage and saw Elliot's heavy frame against the side of the building.

I tried to sit up, but my arms and legs didn't respond; at least, not right away. What should have been a sit up was more of a spasm. I tried again and got my knees under me. Elliot was no longer visible when I got to my feet. The five feet separating me from the tan Nissan Sentra took half a minute to traverse. It was impossible to lift my legs more than a few inches off the ground, so I had to work at driving my shins straight through the snow. I tried to open the car door, but my fingers wouldn't respond to my brain's commands. I tried again and again, but got nowhere. When I heard the first shot, I gave up on the handle. I lifted my arm, pivoted my hips, and drove my elbow into the driver's side window. My arm bounced off the glass, and I fell onto my ass.

I heard another shot as I climbed to my feet. I looked at my hands; the cold had left them limp and useless, and I didn't have time to do anything about it. I braced myself and leaned back as far as I could without falling. When I reached my limit, I leaned forward taking my weight on shaky legs. I repeated the motion, building up shaky momentum as I moved back and forth. When I had enough momentum to make up for my lack of strength, I gritted my teeth and drove my body forward — hard. My head collided with the window and made a hole the size of my forehead in the glass. The window pebbled where I struck it and the glass fell into the car. I put two hands against the car and fought to stay standing. Ignoring the stars I was seeing, I tried my elbow again. The hole had weakened the glass enough for me to knock out a larger hole with my elbow. I clumsily jammed my arm through the hole and began searching for the handle; it was the feeling that was the problem — I couldn't feel anything. I used my elbow to knock out the rest of the glass and then forced my torso into the window. Gravity was the only friend I had in the world, and she pulled me the rest of the way in.

I had to wriggle through the window, and the awkward motion spilled me onto the body in the passenger seat. Diego was slumped forward against the dashboard with a neat hole in the side of his head. I ignored the body and focused on the dashboard. The dials said heat was coming out of the dashboard vents. I slapped my palms against them and held them there while I positioned my foot on the gas.

I heard two more shots, and then, seconds later, another *bang* came from the garage. My hands had begun to hurt, but they had also started moving. I tested moving the gearshift and found I could get the Sentra into drive. I put both hands on the wheel and waited. Someone was going to leave the garage, and I was ready for them with the only weapon available — a Japanese import with worn snow tires.

As minutes ticked by on the dashboard clock, my body began to shake uncontrollably as it fought to regain the heat it lost. My guts ached, but my hands weren't yet ready to explore the wound. I needed more time before I attempted anything that required fine motor skills. I looked beside me at Diego #1 and wondered where Elliot had left his brother's body. I took a hand off the vent and pawed at Diego. I didn't think Elliot would have left anything of value on him, but I had to be sure. I didn't find anything useful on Diego, but while I was going through his pockets I noticed a duffel bag in the back seat. I tried to bring the bag forward, but it was heavy and the effort put a strain on my stomach that sent a searing pain through my torso. I checked the garage; the only thing I could see was light spilling through the open door and onto the snow. I wiggled my fingers and watched as they painfully responded to my instructions. I didn't waste any time lifting my shirt. It was dark in the car, but I didn't need the light; the bullet hole wouldn't tell me anything, but the placement would speak volumes. The closer the hole was to the centre of my body, the worse things would be. I leaned back and grunted through the pain. I wiped away the blood with the edge of my hand and saw a small circle that was darker than everything else in the car — it was three inches above my hip bone. I laughed and it hurt, but I kept laughing. The bullet wouldn't kill me; at least, not right away. Ahead of me, the light on the snow flickered as a black Toyota nosed out the door. Everything that needed to be settled with bullets was done, and it was finally time for the getaway.

Almost.

CHAPTER FIFTY-SEVEN

Elliot had chosen wisely. This car was small, but the snow tires were good. The Sentra's wheels spun for a second and then it began to rapidly pick up speed. The back end began to swing to the right, but the small change in direction didn't matter when I was so close to the target.

The Toyota was halfway out the door when my Nissan hit the passenger's side and drove it into the side of the garage door. I had been aiming for the tire, but I settled for the T-bone. For a split second, I saw the driver's form react in surprise to the oncoming Nissan, and then the impact drove whoever it was into the side window.

I backed up and floored the car into the Toyota a second time. This time, the Nissan didn't drift — it was a perfect line drive. The airbags exploded violently in stereo like a sudden savage magic trick and obscured what I could see of the other car. I put the car in park and slipped past the already deflating bag. I reached in through the shattered passenger window and opened the door. My hands had baked long enough on the vent to accomplish the task on the first try.

Whoever had been driving wasn't visible behind the airbags, but I saw the two duffel bags on the passenger seat. I took the bags and put them in the back seat of the Nissan. On my way back to the Toyota, I ran my eyes over the interior of the garage. Miles wasn't on the floor anymore — Elliot had taken his place. I changed my heading and walked to the pudgy body on the concrete and the pistol still in his hand. I picked up the gun before I looked over the body. Elliot had two holes in his chest that were making a wet sucking sound. A little while ago, our roles had been reversed and Elliot made the clever decision to leave me for dead — I was tired of being clever. I pointed the gun at his head and stole what little time he had left on this earth.

I walked back to the Toyota and looked inside. The airbag had deflated, and I could see Monica low in the driver's seat. She was alive, but unconscious. She had settled her score; I pointed the gun and settled mine.

"You going to kill me, too?"

I stepped back and opened the rear door. Miles was on the floor with his belt wrapped around his leg just above the knee. "You going to make it?"

"I'll make it to trial if you leave me laying here."

I put the gun away and held out my hand. When he was out of the car, Miles steadied himself on my shoulder and looked inside at Monica. "You didn't have to kill her," he said.

"Would you have done it?"

Miles shook his head.

"Then yeah, I did."

"She wasn't a bad person; she just couldn't get past what

happened to her."

"The past was the problem. She was a getaway driver who couldn't get away."

"We brought her back too soon. She wasn't ready for this."

I shook my head. "What happened changed her. She wasn't part of our crew anymore. Monica was just another player on an already crowded board. She was playing her own game with her own set of rules and her own stakes."

Miles groaned as he adjusted his weight. "So this is what winning feels like?"

"You think winning should make you feel like you want to go to Disneyland."

Miles shrugged the shoulder that wasn't resting on me. "It shouldn't feel like this."

"That place is for quarterbacks who win games with rules and referees. That isn't any kind of place for people like us. The games we play are never fair and they never end clean. They just end."

"I guess that's something."

"It's enough. Are you ready to walk away from this?"

Miles looked at his leg. He laughed and then he groaned. "I won't be ready to walk for a while, but I'm ready to go."

I tightened my grip on Miles and turned him towards the Nissan. I opened the door and Miles managed to get himself inside. When I got behind the wheel, he was pulling his leg into the car.

He slammed the door and leaned back against the headrest. "Y'know, there's nothing that says we can't go to Disneyland."

I backed the car up and experimented with turning the wheel. The tires responded the way they should have. "You want to go to Magic Kingdom?"

"We won. I think it is a natural progression. Plus, there are thousands of people in and out every day. It's the perfect place to lay low."

"You really think you'd blend in at the happiest place on earth?"

Miles went quiet and closed his eyes. I thought he had dropped it; then he spoke without looking at anything. "Where do we go? Where do guys like us go after we win?"

"Forward," I said. "We go forward one step at a time. We'll start with a doctor and then find Donny."

Miles laughed. "Do you really think that little shit is going to help us after what you did to him?"

"We'll find out," I said. "We have enough carats to deal with a ton of bad blood."

"And if he's not moved by our haul?"

"We can find someone else," I said. "Or I could shoot him again."

Miles sighed. "You think it will come to that?"

"No. We have something better than cash to a man like Donny."

"Rocks beat paper," Miles said.

"They do. They also forgive a multitude of sins. If you have enough of them."

"Rocks or sins?"

I looked at Miles and then at the bags in the back seat. "Take your pick. We've got plenty of both."